EVERY INCH A LADY

by the same author

TO MAKE AN UNDERWORLD
HOW TO LIVE DANGEROUSLY
YOU WON'T LET ME FINNISH
ALAS POOR FATHER
GRIM DEATH AND THE BARROW BOYS
YOUNG MAN, I THINK YOU'RE DYING
HELL'S BELLE
KILL OR CURE
NO BONES ABOUT IT
MIDNIGHT HAG
NOTHING IS THE NUMBER WHEN YOU DIE
THE CHILL AND THE KILL
DEATH OF A SARDINE
WHEN I GROW RICH
IN THE RED
THE MAN FROM NOWHERE
MISS BONES
MALICE MATRIMONIAL
MAIDEN'S PRAYER
YOU CAN'T BELIEVE YOUR EYES

EVERY INCH A LADY

A MURDER OF THE FIFTIES BY

JOAN FLEMING

G.P. Putnam's Sons · NEW YORK

FIRST AMERICAN EDITION 1977
Copyright © 1977 by Joan Fleming
All rights reserved. This book, or parts thereof, may not be
reproduced in any form without permission.

SBN: 399-12087-4

Library of Congress Cataloging in Publication Data
Fleming, Joan Margaret
   Every inch a lady.
   I. Title.
PZ3.F62845Ev   1977   [PR6011.46]   823'.9'14   77-10423

Lyrics from the following songs are reprinted by permission:
"You're the Cream in my Coffee" © 1928 by DeSylva, Brown and Henderson, Inc. Copyright Renewed. Assigned to Chappell & Co., Inc. International Copyright secured. ALL RIGHTS RESERVED. Used by permission.
"Button Up Your Overcoat" © 1928 by DeSylva, Brown and Henderson, Inc. Copyright Renewed. Assigned to Chappell & Co., Inc. International Copyright secured. ALL RIGHTS RESERVED. Used by permission.

PRINTED IN THE UNITED STATES OF AMERICA

EVERY INCH A LADY

The First Part

CHAPTER I

'What a life!' Police Constable Bacon blew thoughtfully upon his tea and sighed heavily. He had already told his wife a trifle sharply to turn off the television; she gave him a keen look.

'Life's no joke!' he said heavily a few minutes later.

The arrival of a plate of fried fish and chips in front of him interrupted his philosophizing; he gave it a sickened looked, pushed it aside and asked for more tea.

'It's not like me to be put off me oats,' he observed, 'but it's been a nasty day. Very nasty. I reckon I never ought to of been a policeman,' he mused.

'What's got into you, Sam Bacon?'

'I'm getting a sissy in me old age.' Bacon smiled at the absurdity of his suggestion. 'I've seen some sights in my time, but honest, I've never seen nothing what got me like today's job.'

He took a long draught of tea. 'It's all over the evening papers. And it'll be tomorrow's murder, so I'm not giving nothing away when I tell you there's been a slap-up, full-dress murder, with all the knobs on, in one of those posh new houses on the edge of the heath. Putney's never known anything like it, not in my time it hasn't. What a job!'

Mrs Bacon disapproved of shop-talk; she took a pride in the sanctity of her home and liked to feel that when Sam came home he left his work behind him. She now felt, however, that this was the moment for a wife's sympathy and understanding. She popped the plate of fish and chips back into the oven, turned the gas to its lowest, and sat down at the table with an expression of receptive interest.

'Life's a terrible thing,' he told her. 'Why should such things happen to them more than to you and me? Oh, I know they're rich and all that, but all the time I was standing there, on duty, I was thinking: "Here's a couple just like Doris and me!" They've not been married so long; the wife's only a kid and a nice one at that. It went to my heart to see her, straight it did. In the midst of life we are in death, amen.'

During the pause Mrs Bacon made another, this time successful, essay with the fish and chips. But when the meal was over her husband's mood was still heavily lugubrious.

'He was savaged,' he said at last, 'stabbed all over the back like he was a pin-cushion, and the stuffing coming out,' he added, looking awed by his own description.

'Sam Bacon!' his wife cried. 'I don't want no talk of that sort in this house, I don't!'

'You're a funny girl,' Sam said good-naturedly; 'spend hours reading them shocking murder stories and then, when you get a bit of real life, you come all over nice. Upon my word, standing there looking at the horrible scene I thought: this is like one of Doris's bits of literature; *Death of a Fat Man* we'll call this one.'

'But those stories I read are all a bit of fun. Things like that don't happen.'

'Oh, don't they!' Sam stirred his large frame uneasily. 'Don't they! Except that there's one happened last night not a couple of miles from here!'

Interest having worked its way through her prejudices, his wife asked: 'Robbery with violence? Armed robbery, or what?'

'No robbery. All violence. At least no robbery as we could see. No forced entry as we could see. Nothing taken as far as the wife was able to say. It was like this. They've been married six months, this young couple; husband around thirty-two; wife, say, twenty-four. They asked another couple in for cocktails, seeing it was the six months' anniversary of their wedding, and the chap they asked having been their best man, like. The idea was that after they'd finished having their cocktails they'd drive up West for a meal, see? The four of them. Then the husband backed out, said he was too tired, maybe drunk too much, said he didn't feel like it, so off he goes, presumably, to bed, and the other three say ta ta, and off they goes up West, has dinner, goes to a show. The friends bring the wife home in their car, say good night to her on the doorstep; she says come in and have a drink, they say no thanks, it's late. Wife goes upstairs – they've no servants, by the way – looks into her husband's room . . .'

'Husband's room! Don't they sleep together?'

'Posh folk don't; not all night they don't. The husband has what they call a dressing-room, with a bed in it, in which, I presume,' Bacon said primly, 'he sleeps. Don't laugh, Doris, this is no laughing matter. Wife listens outside husband's door, all silent, she opens it a crack, light out, silence, everything okey dokey, she goes off to bed keeping as quiet as she can so's not to disturb her husband. See? Wife sleeps late. The husband usually wakes her with a cuppa tea, but today no one wakes her so she sleeps on. Arrival at nine ack emma of Mrs Whozit, the lady help, who lets herself in with her own key. No breakfast remains, nothing to wash up. Mrs Whozit guesses they've overslept, goes upstairs, wakens wife, pulls back curtains, excetra. Goes into husband's room and what does she find? Darkness, curtains drawn close. She draws back curtains and very near faints. In fact, when we got there she was in hysterics.'

'Dead?' Mrs Bacon whispered.

'Dead! But not only dead . . . he was lying with his head inside the open wardrobe, which is one of those big built-in things they have in these modern houses; he'd fallen down half inside the wardrobe as though he'd been attacked from behind just as he was stooping down to get something out. There was some travel kit underneath him when we moved him at last, and it looks like he'd been getting it out. But his back, Doris! There was stab wounds all over it, through the stuff of his suit; it was like someone had stabbed him over and over again like Grandma used to prod the top of her cottage loaves before she put them to rise. He's a great hefty chap, fifteen stone or more; it took four of us to lift him when they'd finished taking photographs. And then we found the canvas grip and the case underneath him, soaked in blood. It wasn't that that upset me, oh no,' Bacon explained. 'I'm used to the sight of blood, I got over that long ago. It was the young wife and the way I kept thinking it was like you and me, and how you'd carry on if it was me'd been found murdered. She's just a slip of a little thing, Doris, no more than a kid. She was that brave, I'd have been proud of her if she'd been mine. Which she ain't,' he added hurriedly.

'You could see her heart was well nigh broke but she kept a marvellous hold of herself: "Yes, Officer, no, Officer." She was white like a sheet of paper; it would of killed you to see her and how she was trying to keep up. And then the father-in-law turned up, in a bloomin' great old-fashioned Rolls-Royce. I've never seen a man take on like it. They had to go to one of those blocks of "ar-la" flats behind the Ritz in Piccadilly to find him, and he insisted on coming right away. He's a shipping magnate, so they tell me, and this here chap was his only son. He acted like a madman. Pandemonium! Sir Jason bloomin' Cragg, they call him, and he's not that old to be the father of a son of thirty-odd. Good-lookin' chap too, when he's normal.'

'Who do they reckon done it?'

'No idea at all. Between you and me, Doris, I could see my old man was flummoxed, though he looked as though he'd got a lot of private information up his sleeve. They went around looking busy, taking fingerprints on door-knobs, on handrail of the stairs, excetra. But I'd have laughed if I hadn't been upset. They'll get nothing. Whoever did it entered that house with a view to doing it. There was no row nor nothing, no fight. This chap went in with a pair of kid gloves and a sharp knife, did his job and got out, quick as quick.'

'But you said there was no sign of entry.'

'I said, nothing we could find. To me, in confidence, it looks like it was a chap he knew called after the others had gone off to the West End. Maybe he was waiting outside the house in the dark, watching until he knew the Cragg chap was alone, then ringing the bell and being let in normal, like. Maybe the Cragg chap was expecting him. That's my view, anyway, and for why? Because Doris, my love, he was fully dressed. Said he'd stay at home to go to bed, but did he? Not he. Just up your street, eh, ain't it?'

'Do they reckon they know how long he'd been dead?'

'Only rough, very rough. The central heating was on, they've got one of them expensive oil-heating outfits, and the place is like a bloomin' oven. Makes it difficult to estimate exactly how long a body's been a corpse, if you get me.'

'Well, dear me,' Mrs Bacon murmured thoughtfully.

'There's a group of those new houses, all alike but very exclusive, built in what used to be the grounds of that big mansion called Silverdale they pulled down a year or so back, remember? They're called Silverdale, One, Two, Three and Four. And there's a block of service flats, Nero Court, very modern, what actually overlooks the back of the Craggs' house. Today they've been to the other houses, asking questions, and tomorrow, I believe, we're going right through that block of flats with a fine-tooth comb, asking if anyone knew the couple, heard any unusual noise, saw anything funny. There'll be the usual busybodies say they've seen this, heard that, we'll spend hours interviewing thousands, and it'll all add up to nothing, you'll see. A dark night, everyone indoors watching the TV. Anything could happen. Not long ago there was a so-called furniture van went to one of those grand houses, on the other side of the heath it was, some time after business hours; the chaps broke in, all dressed in their white coats like real removal men, and they took every rag and stick out of that house, and there wasn't a soul noticed them, or if they did, thought there was anything up. So what hope have you of finding the murderer? None whatever, though it wouldn't do for anyone to hear me say so. Progress, that's what we're supposed to have, with police cars fitted up with radio so's they can be on the spot before you can count sixty. But the job's done by that time. There's nothing to touch the old bobby on the beat, believe me. He sees a chap lurking round aimless, takes a sharp look at him, passes again to see if he's still there, and if he is, he wonders, and if he's not – then he still wonders. And when a member of the police force starts wondering, well, that's something, anyway. He'll remember that face; maybe he'll never have to, but one in twenty times, maybe, he'll be shown the photographs at the Yard: "Is it any of these?" "Yes," he'll say, "it's that one." And it's in the bag! Progress . . .'

Police Constable Bacon had talked himself into a state of comfort. Mrs Bacon went to wash up and left him musing upon the horrors of progress.

CHAPTER II

She lay face-downwards on the bed, listening to the sound of policemen tramping up and down the polished stairs, of motor cars stopping and starting, the sound of lowered voices, the policeman at the door talking to the visiting reporters. The policewoman was kind, frequently bringing her cups of tea and having little friendly chats about nothing. 'Now you must try not to think about it, dear.

Your husband is out of pain. You must be brave. Try to bear up for his sake.'

The short winter day drew to its close about five o'clock and the darkness put an end to police activity out of doors; the police cars drove away leaving two police constables on duty in the stricken house.

Sir Jason, heavily under the influence of the tranquillizing tablets he had been taking at frequent intervals, tapped on the door.

'May I come in, Easter?'

She raised her head and turned over, her face blotched with red from pressure against her arms.

'My poor dear girl,' he said gently, 'get some night things into a bag and let's go.'

'Go?'

'Yes, you're to come back to Arlington Street with me; I've made arrangements.'

Easter shook her head. 'No, thanks.'

'No nonsense, child. Of course you're coming.'

'No, I'm not, really. Thank you, but . . . this is my home; in spite of everything, I still regard it as my home. I don't want to leave here, Jason, truly.'

'You can't possibly stay here after what's happened,' he told her sharply.

'They're leaving a policeman to guard the house, aren't they?'

He nodded, on the verge of argument.

'Well, then,' Easter said reasonably, 'I shall be quite all right; don't worry about me.'

'Look here, it's impossible to leave you here alone . . .'

'Oh, don't *fuss*,' she said irritably.

He looked searchingly at the ravaged young face. 'Very well, if that's the way you feel about it . . . I shall find a pair of York's pyjamas and sleep in the guest room, not that I shall sleep!'

'There's no need for it,' Easter protested.

He sat down on the edge of the bed and took her limp hand. 'Look, you and I have only got each other now; you've no other relative in the world, have you?'

She did not answer but looked away.

'Have you?' he urged, shaking her hand. 'And I've only my club friends, business friends and acquaintances; it is blood relations that matter at a time like this, and you're the nearest thing I have to that. Besides, I feel . . . there's nothing left of my poor boy but you. We must stick together, Easter, it is the only comfort we shall have; that and . . . bringing whoever did it to justice. Up to now I've been a firm abolitionist but, my God, it makes you wonder. It's easy to talk about abolishing hanging so long as your only son hasn't been murdered. But when he has –' he coughed – 'when he has . . . hanging seems a lot too good for the bloke that did this. Practical experience makes all the difference,' he added wryly.

He went across to the window and drew aside the heavy lined curtain, looked out into the darkness for a minute. Sir Jason Cragg was of the same build as his son, York, had been; not tall, he was powerfully built and well covered so that it would not take much in the way of excess to make him a fat man. That he was well tailored and well groomed afforded him protection from that description as a rule, but upon this particular evening there was no doubt that he looked a distracted fat man. He peered this way and that into the darkness.

'Who knows? He may be watching the house, like the proverbial dog returning to its vomit. He may be out there now, crouching in the bushes, watching and waiting, or he may have been disturbed at his task when you came back, Easter. Or perhaps he lay hidden in the darkness somewhere in the house, waiting for an opportunity to look round. Or, when he saw that it was hopeless without waking you with sound and lights, he may have let himself out by the front door, planning to come back some other time, when the house was deserted.'

'Oh, do stop it!' she cried. 'Are you trying to frighten me, or what?'

'But if he comes back,' Sir Jason went on discursively, '*I* shall kill *him*; it will be my turn.'

He let the curtain drop back into place and picked up the photograph of his son from the dressing-table. He stared at it for a long time. Then he went slowly from the room without another word.

CHAPTER III

John Ramsgate had been at Cambridge with York Cragg and was now a member of Lloyd's. Both he and his wife Jill were able to give a full and frank description of the evening they had spent. The Ramsgates had two young children, one of whom had whooping cough; on the evening of the murder, this child had had some bad paroxysms of coughing and the nannie had stayed up in order to talk to the father and mother on their return about the desirability of asking the doctor to come at that late hour to give the child something to calm him and so enable everyone in the house to get some sleep. There was, therefore, no question as to what hour the young couple had returned home; the doctor was telephoned for within a few minutes of their return, he came at once, and the child was attended to in the presence of his father and mother.

Since the movements of everyone connected in any way with the crime had to be checked, the Ramsgates were able to produce a couple of acquaintances who corroborated the fact that they had met the Ramsgates and Easter Cragg as they came out of the Windmill Theatre together not long after eleven.

At about seven-fifteen, York Cragg had telephoned to

his father, it being a few minutes after his wife and the Ramsgates had left the house. He had arranged with his father to go to Southampton the following morning to meet the *Queen Elizabeth* which was arriving from New York with an important client of the Golden Fleece Shipping Company on board. His father was, within a minute or two, in no doubt as to the time his son had telephoned; he had been expecting a friend to dine with him in Arlington Street at seven-fifteen, and was keeping an eye on the clock as he spoke to his son on the telephone.

The staff of a Hungarian restaurant in the West End had no difficulty at all in remembering the couple who, in the company of a second young woman, dined there before going on to the theatre.

York Cragg, therefore, had been alive at seven-fifteen, some fifteen minutes after his wife and friends had left the house; some time between then and nine o'clock the following morning, he had been murdered. The police discounted the possibility of his having been killed within at least four hours of his body having been found.

As Mrs Cragg had been at home from midnight onwards and would have heard any unusual noise, it was fairly safe to assume that Cragg was killed some time between the time of the telephone call, seven-fifteen, and the return of his wife, midnight.

Starting with these premises, the following morning then, the police began their more intimate questioning: 'I do want you to understand, Mrs Cragg, that we are, if anything, more anxious than you to bring this criminal to justice and that everything you can possibly tell us about your husband's private life may be of value. Sir Jason will, we assume, be able to give us any information there may be with regard to his business life, but I must rely on you for the rest.'

'I'm afraid there is very little I can tell you, Officer. I do assure you — ' she smiled a little wanly — 'that my husband did not lead a double life. I think I can safely say I knew everything about him.'

'Ah, yes.' The inspector looked thoughtful as his assistant scribbled busily in his notebook.

'We went racing from time to time, but don't get the idea that he was heavily involved; it was only for pleasure. You will see from his bank statements that everything was above board. My father-in-law, Sir Jason, paid a generous salary to my husband for his services to the Golden Fleece.'

'Shipping company, that is.'

'What? Er . . . yes . . . of course. The Golden Fleece Shipping Company.'

'What about friends?'

'John Ramsgate was his best friend. As for the others . . . well . . . we had the usual group of friends, mostly young people. If you like I can look out the list of people we asked to our Christmas Eve party; about thirty of them. But I don't think you'll find any of them are possible murderers, Inspector.'

'Anyone, my dear young lady, is a possible murderer; and someone,' he said cryptically, 'is a positive one. You see, your husband *has* been murdered; therefore, someone murdered him. It's as easy as that.'

'Easy!' she repeated thoughtfully. 'I think you will find, Inspector, that this will turn out to be a crime without a motive. My husband wasn't blackmailing anyone, he wasn't the possessor of valuable jewels or documents, he wasn't an heir to a fortune, he wasn't the father of an illegitimate unborn baby, he wasn't a homosexual, he wasn't even – ' she said with the ghost of a smile, ' – an identical twin. And motiveless crimes are so much less easy to solve, aren't they?'

The inspector remained impassive. 'There's something you've left out,' he reminded her gently, 'the "friend" sent to gaol for a crime which he did not commit who, when he is released, hurries to take the vengeance he has vowed during the years of imprisonment towards the really guilty man.'

'You won't find that, either,' she returned equally gently; 'he was incorruptible, incorrupted.'

'Yes, Mrs Cragg. But you don't really expect me to take your word for it, do you? I shall investigate all the possibilities you have suggested because, you see, as I have just reminded you, he *was* murdered, so there *must* have been a motive.'

She simply shrugged and waited patiently for more questions.

Later the inspector said: 'She's a very remarkable young woman, that Mrs Cragg. They tell me she was an air hostess; if I was falling through the sky in a burning plane and I had her hand to hold, it would help, believe me, it would!'

CHAPTER IV

'My son and his wife adored each other,' Sir Jason told the police. 'From the moment they met, ski-ing in Austria, they were just like that.' He clasped his hands together to show how close the couple were. 'I knew York would never marry until he felt he had found the girl he really wanted. He was run after quite considerably by pretty girls and their fond mamas. Once or twice, it looked as though he were falling, but it never came to anything. I was anxious for him to marry, naturally, I want . . . wanted a grandson. I asked York more than once when he was going to marry and he always answered: "When I meet the right girl, Dad!" Finally he met my daughter-in-law last spring at St Anton, floundering about, so I am told, in the snow. She was never any good at ski-ing; my son was first class in spite of his build. Well, there it was. They knew each other out there for, let me see, about a fortnight. York brought her to see me as soon as they got home; it was hardly to ask my permission to get married, but it was a gesture which I appreciated. I took to her at once, who wouldn't? She's a great gal; she's got everything, looks, character, ability. She'd no money, of course, but, fortunately, it didn't matter about that. One thing – I'm perfectly certain she didn't marry York for his money; she's not like that.'

'They were married shortly after?'

'No; my daughter-in-law worked for an airline as air hostess; she had to give reasonable notice of her intention to leave. And then, of course, there was a house or flat to be found and furnished. Altogether they were engaged for about six months, and during that time, as I got to know her better, I realized that my son had picked a fine gal. I was delighted. I bought them this house as a wedding present. They were married, let's see, yes, it was at the end of July; they flew to the South of France for a honeymoon. Since then one has had every reason to suppose that it was a successful marriage. I mean, there wasn't any doubt about it that those two were wrapped up in each other. I have no doubt that it has passed through your mind, Inspector, that my son led a double life; but, believe me, he didn't. He was one of the most candid, open, yes, *uncomplicated* people you could meet.'

The inspector nodded thoughtfully. 'That is the impression of your son that one has,' he agreed, 'but . . .'

'But he was murdered!'

CHAPTER V

Imprisoned in every fat man, we are told, is a thin one wildly signalling to be let out. But the thin man in Sir Jason Cragg, chairman of the Golden Fleece Shipping Company, worn out with wild signalling, had within recent years become a weary, attenuated creature, waving feebly, hope spent. Sir Jason, madly successful, had reached the top of his particular tree, or mast, at the early age of forty, after which he had nothing more for which to strive, and nothing to which he could look forward other than thirty years of being an extremely rich, successful man. Though he bustled about, flying to America and back by Pan American Airways, hurtling around Europe by BEA, playing golf at Gleneagles, the thin man in him felt lonely and frustrated.

In his large, cheerful and altogether successful face were two pale brown sad eyes, like the eyes of a small dog with a lovely nature but, through no fault of his own, an anomalous body.

By the natural law of things-as-they-are, Sir Jason's son should have turned out to be a wastrel, a minor poet or an unsuccessful artist; but nothing of the sort occurred. York seemed to be as perfect a son as any man could possibly wish. He studied Law at Cambridge, got a good second-class degree and went straight into the firm where, with his great charm of manner, he made a splendid representative.

So well did his son turn out that Sir Jason began, almost unconsciously, to be slightly bored; he longed for his son to marry and to produce a son of his own. Secretly, Sir Jason fancied himself as the benevolent grandfather, getting his grandson out of innumerable scrapes, paying his debts and doling out sly advice as to the way to deal with women.

But what did it all add up to Sir Jason asked himself, lying back in the comfortable arms of a hired limousine as it purred back from the crematorium. *'Funeral private, no flowers and no letters, please.'*

If only York could have been killed in that last exciting year of the war when he had been in the RAF and flown over the British Expeditionary Forces at the landing on the Normandy beaches on D-Day! How proudly he would have borne the memory of his hero son for the rest of his life!

He looked at his daughter-in-law, silent and forlorn, sitting unhappy beside him in the motor car, looking out through the steamy window, seeing nothing. One hand was lying limply by her side; Sir Jason picked it up and turned it over, looking thoughtfully into the pink, shell-like palm with the fingers curled over it like petals.

'What a useless little hand,' he said tenderly. He studied her slender wrist upon which she wore four jingly silver bracelets. 'Poor little Easter,' he murmured.

'Don't, please don't be kind or I shall cry.'

'Why not? You haven't cried at all, child. It would do you good.' He was thinking: what a pity she's not going to have a baby, it would make all the difference, to us both; it would be something to live for.

He looked from her wrist to her slender ankles and neatly-shod feet, the long smooth legs, the brief tight skirt, the well-fitting jacket, her small set face, white and stern, her smooth unwaved hair, and her unlined brow, her closed eyes with the full childish lids. She had a faintly expensive smell.

Sir Jason turned his head away and closed his eyes. I could easily, he thought, marry her and have another son. Perhaps, in time, when she has recovered from the shock ... But the thin man wilted in sheer amazement. It would be like committing incest! To marry his own darling daughter-in-law! Sir Jason whipped out his clean pocket handkerchief and hastily passed it over his immaculate brow. What a lecherous old horror he was becoming; men of his age, he had heard, were sometimes taken with strangely uncouth, even lubricous ideas; he must take care.

'We'll have a bite of something to eat in Arlington Street and then I'll send you home.'

'Thank you.'

'That is, if you insist. But you know, Easter, what I feel about that. I am very much against your continuing to live in that house.'

'If you could only understand.'

'Understand what?'

'Understand just how much my home means to me. You know the sort of upbringing I had; the only home life I've ever known is since I've been married. I love my house, my furniture, my own bed. And I feel safe there . . . oddly enough,' she added.

'To my mind, love, it's not the house that makes the home, it's the people in it, and the . . . let's say the affection and trust between those people. If you came to live with me in Arlington Street, for instance . . .'

Easter turned her head sharply, frowning. 'You can't be serious!'

'Why not?'

She fell silent for a full minute. 'It wouldn't do,' she said at last. 'You're not exactly an elderly father-in-law, Jason.'

'Indeed I am!'

'Fifty-seven?' she asked mockingly. 'No wonder I've never been able to call you "Dad". I wonder why you married so young!'

'Because I met the Right Girl and because her father happened to be a successful ship-owner. I didn't marry her for money, though I must admit,' he mused, 'I did go where money was! I've been a widower for so long now,' he said wistfully; 'I felt myself an elderly man at twenty-five.' He lapsed into thought.

'The chairman of the Golden Fleece Shipping Company and his young daughter-in-law . . . no, it wouldn't do. People are unkind. If you think it over you'll see that for me to go back to Putney and be on my own is the only thing. It isn't as though I mind being on my own . . .' she shrugged. 'Since York had to be taken from me there's nobody else I *can* live with, is there?' There was a pause. 'Is there?' she repeated.

'I suppose not.'

'Well, then.'

They were silent until they arrived at the entrance to Sir Jason's extremely luxurious flat.

'Wait to take Mrs York back to Putney,' Sir Jason told the chauffeur as he hoisted himself out of the car.

'I don't know why,' he said later as he removed the wire and gold paper from the top of a champagne bottle, 'I don't know why people always keep champagne for joyful occasions. I believe in opening a bottle of champagne when life's perfectly bloody.' He poured the wine. 'Well, Easter, here's to you and me! You and me! This terrible thing has happened to us and here we both are, getting around, keeping going, keeping up appearances, as they say. We could go mad, knock things about, scream and tear our hair, and I dare say if our juices were arranged differently, that's what we'd be doing. As it is . . .' He drained his glass and poured more wine into it. 'You're wonderful, Easter. You're a woman in a million, my dear. I'm proud of you, and York would be proud of you.' He wandered restlessly across to the window. 'All this searching for the weapon! What a lot of rot it is; what a waste of the country's money. I actually told the inspector chap as much. I said: "There's nothing easier to hide, or dispose of, than a dagger, knife or stiletto. A chap can clean the blade on some cotton wool, his pocket handkerchief, or, in fact, any rag of material, pull the plug on it and slip the knife into his trousers' pocket. Wrap something round the blade and you could slip a knife with a six-inch blade into a trousers' pocket easily. And as for final disposing of a knife, what could possibly be easier than the Thames? This chap that . . . this murderer of ours, Easter, could easily have stopped his car, let down the window and chucked it over Putney Bridge into the river. Or down a street drain. Or under floorboards in any house or flat. Or plunge it into the ground in any park, on Putney Heath, in Battersea Park, on Brighton Beach. Endless possibilities. Looking for the weapon! Hell!'

Easter was sitting in a chair, her long, lovely legs coiled sideways, holding her empty glass.

'The thing is,' her father-in-law went on, 'the police have their methods, their routine methods, I should say, and they've got to go through the whole boiling, in a murder of any kind. But seventy-five per cent of their efforts are wasted in a lot of cases, this, for one. On the surface this murder looks so simple; every gangling youth these days has his dagger on him. Every Monday morning brings newspaper reports of the weekend's stabbing case. If York didn't happen to be who he was, I doubt if it would have raised any interest at all; a tiny paragraph in the national dailies and that's the lot! As it is, you will have noticed how the case has already been relegated to the smallest possible paragraph. There'll probably be a photograph in the cheaper press tomorrow, of you and me walking away from the crematorium, and that will be that. Yes, it is the simplest possible murder, on the face of it. The police, of course, don't believe for one moment that York was the golden-headed boy we make him out to be. I'm pretty sure they think that, once you were out of the house, York, having telephoned dutifully to his father, made off to some disreputable night-club or pub, got thoroughly drunk, got into some dispute with a thug who followed him back home and stabbed him then and there. There was a good deal of alcohol inside him, you'll remember.'

'But that was accounted for by the celebration we'd just been having.'

'Yes, Easter, and no doubt the Ramsgates' stomachs would have shown an equal amount.'

'And mine.'

'And yours. It was a cold night, a cold winter's night; even a thug would be wearing gloves to keep his hands warm, apart from the question of fingerprints. A pair of ordinary wool-lined brown leather gloves! You can stab quite as well in gloves as without them, I'm sure.'

Easter turned her bracelets round and round her wrist. 'Perhaps that's what did happen.'

'Not it,' Sir Jason said firmly. 'People have to act in character. Can you see York slinking out to a club or pub the moment you and the Ramsgates had left the house?'

'I can't. But then, I can't see why York didn't come with us.'

'Eh? What?'

Easter repeated what she had said.

'You can't. Why didn't you say that before?'

'Why should I? What good would it have done?'

'Do you really feel that, Easter?'

She nodded. 'It was exactly six months since we were married. Just an excuse for a party; we'd booked four seats at the Windmill Theatre. John Ramsgate was to be host for the dinner and had already booked a table at the Hungaria. And then, as we're all starting out, what happens? York says he doesn't feel up to it; he's got a cold coming on! I ask you. An attack of flu.'

'What did you have to drink?'

'Champagne cocktails only. I admit we had about three each, but we were only merry; John had no worry about driving, or anything like that. We had some of those little eats from Fortnum's with the wine.'

'Were you surprised, Easter?'

'At what? At his not coming with us? I was astonished, and a bit worried too. I tried not to show it, but I had a hell of an evening worrying, wondering what was really wrong with him, wondering if he was going to be ill, or anything. And when I got home and found everything quiet, his light out and so on, I thought, well, perhaps he really did have a cold; anyway, everything seems all right now. I was thankful the Ramsgates didn't come in, though. I crept off to bed myself and didn't think any more about it.' She paused. 'Since you were talking about "people acting in character" I had to mention that. It certainly wasn't acting in character for York to say he wasn't coming. You know how much he enjoyed everything. He loved an evening out. A cold!'

Sir Jason filled Easter's glass and his own. He raised it to her. 'No, I can't make it a toast, but I solemnly swear that I shall not rest happily, nor allow my mind to be at ease, until I have discovered this murderer and brought him to justice. This crime *will not* go unavenged, Easter, this crime *will not* become just another *Unsolved* crime in the file at Scotland Yard. I shall use all the energy and all the initiative I can muster and, yes, all the money; if necessary, I'll employ a private eye, not your hole-and-corner Peeping Tom, your chappie paid to follow guilty wives or erring husbands. I'll get half the Secret Service on to it, I'll get the Quai des Orfèvres, Interpol . . .'

Suddenly he crumpled on to a chair, and, holding his empty glass between trembling fingers: 'But what's the use? None of it will bring York back.'

Easter uncoiled herself and, coming slowly across the room, she laid a hand on his stout shoulder for a moment, then walked swiftly to the door. With her hand on the knob, she turned to hear him say: 'I'll be along tomorrow morning, if you don't mind, Easter; I'd like to go through his desk, his private papers, bank sheets, and so on . . .'

'Of course . . . Goodbye for now . . . Jason.'

CHAPTER VI

To sort out the personal possessions of the dead is a dreary task, but Sir Jason was no procrastinator; when there was a particularly unpleasant job to be done, he did it as quickly and as soon as possible. Sitting at his son's large flat-topped, leather-covered desk in the small room they called the study, he scanned papers and letters, crumpling up those he thought irrelevant until there was a large pile of waste paper on the floor beside him. He kept photographs: prep-school groups, football teams, house groups, RAF groups, Cambridge rowing crews, amateur theatricals and, finally, photographs of York's wedding. He put these carefully aside, together with bank statements, the deeds of the house, cheque-book stubs and receipts. He made a separate pile of unpaid bills, but there were not many of these; on the whole York was methodical; his affairs were in as good order as those of anyone suddenly snuffed out were likely to be.

Why do people deliberately slip flat objects under the paper which lines the bottom of a drawer when they are not particularly anxious for them to be found? In some drawers, the lining paper invariably slides back, revealing the plain wooden drawer-bottom; and in other types of drawer, the lining paper stays firmly in place for generations. Why bother to slip treasured and private objects under the paper in a private drawer containing personal papers and always kept locked? There isn't a satisfactory answer. It is simply a trick of action or behaviour that occurs in people and is inexplicable; like fussiness about starting to eat a boiled egg at the blunt end, using a hanging chain on a motor car to prevent car-sickness, and passing the port round in a clockwise direction.

If a desk is being ransacked, there is not much chance of something hidden under the lining paper being overlooked; on the other hand, a document thus secreted has been known to turn up after a hundred years of concealment.

There was no earthly reason why Sir Jason should look under the paper of a certain drawer in his son's desk, but the grim fact remains that he did.

One thing is quite clear; the fact that it *was* pushed under the lining paper gave it an importance to which it might not otherwise have been entitled.

It was a shiny photograph of the publicity type, measuring eight by twelve inches. Some people might exclaim at the woman's beauty, others might be equally repelled, but it was certainly a striking photograph. At the bottom was written in stagey sort of writing: 'To my darling York. Your Mavourneen.'

Sir Jason held it at arm's length, as though he had found something extremely revolting: 'Who the hell's this bitch?' he asked aloud.

It was the photograph of a woman of about thirty; she had the usual bust; it was her face that was striking. Her dark hair was drawn tightly upwards, away from her face, the heavy plait was worn like a coronet, her eyes and eyebrows were made up into an exaggerated upward slant and the mouth was a voluptuous monstrosity with an under-lip that never was on land nor sea. One ear only was visible and it was long and pointed, like that of a pixie. The whole was framed in a diaphanous, sari-like stole.

After studying it for some time with an inscrutable expression on his face, Sir Jason slipped it back under the paper where he had found it. He finished his task in the study and went heavily upstairs to sort out his son's clothes. Easter was out; shopping, she had said, but Sir Jason appreciated that she had preferred to leave him alone to his melancholy employment.

They had decided to send all York's clothes to the vicar of a poor East End parish, and with this in mind Sir Jason went through every one of his son's pockets, to make quite sure that no letters, addresses or anything of the kind went with the clothes. He was careful to look under the lining paper of each drawer as he emptied it. When he had finished, he went downstairs again, resolved upon destroying the photograph, tearing it into scraps and burning it on the drawing-room fire.

The police, he knew, had already been through all York's personal possessions, with the exception of the locked drawers of his desk, looking for letters which might be incriminating. Before the search, however, Easter had evidently taken the desk keys into her possession, and she had handed them over to her father-in-law at the funeral; it was understood that if anything relevant to the murder had turned up, Sir Jason would have told the police.

Was it possible, Sir Jason now wondered, that the photograph had any bearing whatever on the murder? Once again he opened the drawers, took out the photograph, propped it up on the chimneypiece and sat down in an armchair.

The impeccable York's past, he thought bitterly. He remembered the emphasis both he and Easter had laid upon their version of York's blameless character to the police. Methinks he doth protest too much, he thought wretchedly. And then: *Et tu, Brute?*

He could so easily tear the photograph into small scraps and burn it along with the pile of irrelevant papers he had been through, and nobody would ever know anything about it. But would he have a happy and comfortable moment after it? To the end of his life he would have to wonder, speculate, imagine ... he would never know.

A lot of fathers would not want to know, they would prefer to forget it. But Jason Cragg was not made like that. He had to know. And so long as he kept the photograph there was a chance of finding out who and what she was; if he destroyed it, he would never know.

He found an envelope large enough to take the photograph and, with shaking fingers, he slipped it inside and put the envelope into his despatch-case.

When Easter returned, he was squatting beside the drawing-room fire, burning papers. He was no dissembler; the wistfulness in his pale brown eyes was replaced by a stolid bewilderment which couldn't be mistaken for anything else.

'You've found it,' Easter said immediately. 'I half hoped you would. It will be a relief to share it; it's been getting me down.' She threw off her mink coat, untied her headscarf and slipped to the floor beside the fire. 'Let's talk about it, Jason, shall we?'

'Who the hell is she?'

'She's somebody he called Mavourneen, possibly not a name, but an Irish term of endearment.'

'I know that much.'

'She's either a minor, very minor actress, or a model-girl, or . . . anyway, I'm sure she earns her living from her looks, one way or another. York has known her for years; she's been The Woman in His Life. No wonder he didn't fancy any of the pretty debs you were so hopeful about, darling.'

Sir Jason heard the darling and looked down at his hands, with her slim hand resting lightly on them, in amazement and with some pleasure.

'I'm not at all sure where she lives, the envelopes and the few letters I found had various postmarks and I hadn't time to study them. She puts "Sat." at the top of her letters, and that's all.'

'Don't tell me there's a child, after all. That would be too, too ordinary.'

'I'm quite sure there isn't. But then she was quite sure that York would marry her.'

'And because he didn't, she had her revenge, coming

along one night when he was alone and stabbing him, ha ha!' Sir Jason said mirthlessly.

'That sort of thing,' Easter nodded unhappily.

'Which would account for his staying at home when you all went to the theatre. Possibly she had said she was coming and he arranged to be alone here at that time. Oh, crikey, what a thing!' he groaned.

'Why do men keep letters?' Easter asked. 'I can't understand *why*. York hadn't kept all her letters, by any means, I'm sure. There were six, two of them only notes. And she couldn't write anyway. I mean, they were the letters of a house-maid! Notes, really, protesting undying love, begging him to see her.'

'You destroyed them?'

'Yes, I did, Jason, I did. I don't want anybody to think that everything wasn't all right between York and me. It was. York had finished with her before he went to St Anton. He was sick to death of her. He told me there "had been a woman" but that it was "all over", and there was no need for me to ask any more. There were times, since we married, when I knew he was worried about something.'

'Didn't you see the letters arriving?'

'There weren't many, Jason. There couldn't have been more than three or four in the last six months. I suppose I could have discovered something about her if I had studied the postmarks, but I was in such a hurry to get them destroyed. You ask if I did not see them arriving? Was I likely to look with suspicion at York's post? He had lots of mail every day, why should I notice particularly those few letters?'

'Why didn't you tear up the photograph too?'

Easter sat back upon her heels. 'Ah, why? That's something I can't answer. Unless . . .'

'Unless what?'

'Don't you see? That she killed York.'

'Weren't you a bit late in coming to that conclusion?'

he asked irritably. 'You destroyed the letters, which might have made it possible to track her down. 'What can we do with this single photograph? There's nothing to go on. You were too hasty in destroying the letters, Easter.'

'Perhaps. Maybe I had a sort of sympathy with her, temporary, of course. The same sort of feeling I had about that platinum blonde, years back, the last woman ever to be hanged, who shot her lover dead as he came out of a pub in Hampstead. Remember?'

'Of course I do. She wanted to be hanged, poor wretch.'

'There you are, you see. You've got some sympathy for her, too.'

'But Easter, my dear, you've compromised. You haven't done either one thing or the other. You destroyed the letters and kept the photograph. I've sworn that York's murderer will be "brought to justice", as they call it. There is nothing I can do other than hand it over to the police.'

'And then all the world will know that I was a "wronged woman",' Easter said. 'The sensational Sunday papers will simply ooze sympathy and point the finger of scorn, as they call it, at the wicked husband who deceived me, or else, the faithless lover who deserted his woman for another. It won't be: "poor York Cragg, who was murdered", it will be: "that wretched York Cragg who had it coming to him".'

'Go on.'

'There's nothing more to it. If we want to damn York in the eyes of the world, all we have to do is to give that photograph to the police. And anyway,' Easter went on, after a pause, 'do you really think a woman could do all that stabbing?'

'If you'd ever done bayonet-practice you'd say yes.'

'Bayonet practice!' Easter cried. 'A straw-stuffed uniform! York was over fifteen stone!'

'Of course a woman might have done it . . .' Jason said soberly. 'Look at Charlotte Corday, for instance. There are ribs in the way, but if you have a sharp enough knife,

Easter, and get between the ribs with the first shot. Oh, hell! What a bloody awful life!'

Easter was thoughtful, twisting her silver bracelets round and round her tiny wrist. 'What are you going to do, then?'

'I must think it over,' Jason said distractedly. 'I will take that damn photograph away and, well, just think it over.'

'Then you didn't mean what you said last night?'

'What did I say last night?'

'After the funeral, about finding out who the murderer was at all costs.'

'I mean every word of it. Dammit, woman, give me a chance.'

'Where is the photograph now?'

'In my despatch-case. I'm taking it away with anything else that has to be kept; bank sheets and so on.'

'Then you are going to do something about it?'

'I don't know.' Jason was in the hall, shrugging himself into his overcoat. 'But I do know that I'm going to make sure there's a police watch kept on this house whilst you are alone here.'

'That won't be the least necessary,' Easter pointed out, 'if who we think did it – *did it*.'

Standing in the hall, heavy despatch-case under his arm, hat in hand, Jason looked at his daughter-in-law. The large, brisk, confident, successful businessman seemed to have merged into something not inferior but different; though more careworn, he was younger, less self-confident, and perplexed.

'Did you really love York?' he asked quietly.

'I thought I did, at first.'

'And then?'

Easter shook her head and said nothing.

'So you didn't love him?' he persisted.

'I thought he was something that he wasn't.'

'How do you mean?'

'He was like you, Jason. He modelled himself on you,

he had some of your mannerisms, he talked like you, behaved like you, up to a point; but there wasn't anything beyond that point. He was an ordinary, ordinary man.'

'I've wondered,' he said, 'why you didn't cry.'

'I'm crying now,' Easter wept in astonishment, 'I'm crying,' she cried, 'because I believe it's you I've loved all the time.'

With his weighty despatch-case in one hand and his bowler hat in the other, he stood, as immobile and ineffectual as a scarecrow. Then her arms were round his neck, she was pressed against him and her face, wet with tears, was rubbing against his own astonished face. He tasted tears. He was quite silent, as though stricken dumb for life. It might have lasted hours, minutes or seconds, he never knew. Somehow, some time, it was over; she turned away from him, still weeping. He stood by the front door, wondering how on earth to get it open and then realizing, with surprise, that he could put his hat into the same hand that held the despatch-case and open the door with the other. It was as easy as that.

The chauffeur closed the door of the car and, as they drew away, Jason shook himself like a large wet bird.

It hadn't, of course, happened.

CHAPTER VII

'Mavourneen,' he kept saying to himself. 'Mavourneen.' It was soft and round and satisfactory, like her breasts.

He went to the City, he had a committee, he interviewed the family solicitor, handing over all that he had taken from York's desk (except the photograph), he had drinks at the Savoy with two business acquaintances, he went to his club for dinner. And all the time he could not let his despatch-case out of his sight. All day he longed to take out the photograph and have another look at it, but not until after midnight, alone in his flat, did he do so.

What a strange, haunting face! The apparent fact York deserted her for the immature schoolgirl who was his wife was material for endless speculation. Easter was a clever girl; she made a fine wife; efficient, intelligent and self-reliant. And she was pretty, with her smooth, shining hair, her long slim legs, her tiny waist. But after the rich wine that was 'Mavourneen', she seemed a draught of lime-juice and water.

Was it possible that Mavourneen had loved York so deeply that, rather than lose him to another woman, she stabbed him to death and thus lost him for ever? If so, his father thought appraisingly, there must have been a lot more to York than one would think. Large, cheerful, athletic, a good dancer, an efficient skier, popular as a cocktail-party guest, a delightful escort; did York really rouse Mavourneen to extremes of primitive passion?

As the night wore on, Jason realized unhappily that his resolve to avenge his son's death was being undermined. It was being replaced by another, far less worthy, resolution. Somehow or other, he would have to find the woman and satisfy himself about her.

He pulled himself out of his armchair and went across to the window, drawing the curtain aside and peering out over the acres of slate roofs to the bare trees of the park. It was a stormy night, with black clouds racing out of the west and the moon playing a coy game of hide and seek. He had a stupid desire to go out and walk about, peering into the face of every woman he might meet.

His mind formed an eldritch advertisement, inserted in *The Times*: 'If Mavourneen with the pointed ears and wonderful eyes will get in touch with the advertiser she will hear something to her advantage.' There was precious little agony in that column of *The Times* these days, but his, at least, would be a cry from the heart. And, of course,

Mavourneen would not see *The Times*.

The obvious, the only sensible thing, was to hand her photograph over to the police who would, in due course, deliver it to the more sensational papers who would publish it on their front pages: 'Friend of the murdered man who, it is believed, can help the police in their enquiries.' 'Have you seen this woman?' 'Who is she?'

It was easy; someone, somewhere, would recognize her. Within a week of giving the photograph to the police, he was sure, he would meet her, see her for himself.

But he remembered the woman in Hampstead whom they had talked about, hanged for shooting her lover: a *crime passionel* which, in France, they virtually condoned. He had always condemned the old 'eye for an eye' rule; how would the punishment, in one way or another, of Mavourneen help his son?

He looked at the long thin neck and shuddered at the thought of the rope round it, knotted below that pixie's ear. No, he mustn't risk that. He had a better idea.

CHAPTER VIII

He was worried about Easter. Though for some days he neither went to Putney to see her, nor did he telephone to her, nevertheless he was worried. Easter had become something of a problem.

The trouble was that, knowing her background, one's opinion of Easter was apt to be confused by a certain pity for her. She had been, as she was inclined to joke, 'born an orphan'. When she was only a few days old, somebody had left the infant girl in a London Roman Catholic Church before High Mass on Easter Sunday. She was handed over to a community of nuns who had brought her up.

There was really no need for much pity; Easter had had a happy childhood and youth. When she reached the requisite age, the nuns sent her to a smart and expensive boarding school run by a branch of their community and in due course she was sent to another branch in Brussels for 'finishing'. Seldom has a foundling been in less need of sympathy. But the fact remained that there was something infinitely appealing, and very nearly pathetic, about Easter now that she was a widow.

The police might be keeping a constant watch on the house, Jason thought, but there she was, all alone in her house with her possessions. The morning woman apparently had not come, not having recovered from the shock; Easter was going through the daily routine of dusting the house, shopping, cooking her own cutlet and going to bed. If she had had a mother or a sister who could have lived with her at this time, one would have felt happier. Nor did she seem to have a particular friend who could come to stay with her.

Perhaps he ought to send her away for a time, into the sunshine. He should insist that she fly to the Bahamas, away from it all, for the time being. Having considered it for a day or two, he rang her up.

'I can't bear the thought of your being down there all alone,' he told her. 'If you won't come here, will you let me arrange for you to fly to the Bahamas? We have an agent out there; I could cable him to get you fixed up in a first-rate hotel. The sunshine, Easter, the change of scene . . .' Sensing a lack of enthusiasm at the other end of the line he tailed off.

'Could you go too?'

Jason hesitated; after all she had primly said about the two of them together in the Arlington Street flat, this was a surprise.

'I would,' he stammered at last, 'I would if it weren't for business. It's not convenient at the moment, as a matter of fact. Whilst this Board of Trade new scheme is unsettled, I'd rather stay at the helm.'

'Then I'd rather stay here and be near you.'

'But you're not so near me.'

Though he could not see it, he knew she was smiling her charming smile; there was a pause during which he could have imagined that she whispered: 'Not so near as I would like to be.'

'What?'

'At the end of a telephone line, Jason, which is better than nothing.'

'Then you won't accept my offer?'

'It's lovely of you, but no, thank you. And by the way ... that photograph. You said you were going to think about it.'

'Yes, and I have been doing so.'

'I don't know what you have decided, but you wouldn't do anything without talking to me first?'

Pause.

'Would you?'

'We can't possibly discuss it on the telephone, Easter.'

'It's just that I'm worried about that photograph. I wish it were destroyed.'

'Would you feel happier if it were?'

'Of course. It's something between you and me.'

'And York.'

'Jason, you're treating it like a scrape York got himself into. It matters terribly to me. Please, please may I have it back?'

'Of course you shall, Easter. I'll bring it back to you and you can do what you like with it.'

'When?'

'In a day or two.'

'Why a day or two?'

'Easter, if it would make you any happier I would tear

it up now. But we've talked it over and I'm still thinking it over. It's been one hell of a shock; it takes time to recover. You are the more pressing worry. It is only under protest I'm leaving you alone down there. Understand, Easter? Under protest.'

She went upstairs to York's dressing-room and stood there for a long time. The policewoman had cleaned up the bottom of the cupboard after the blood-sodden cases had been removed, but there were still darkish, scrubbed-looking patches on the white woodwork of the cupboard's base and on the close-fitting carpet. After a while she peered inside the empty wardrobe; she opened the drawers; they were all empty, but on the dressing-table were York's silver-backed brushes, his leather stud-boxes, a photograph of his long-dead mother. And a photograph of herself in the smart uniform of the airline for which she had worked. She had asked him why he did not put out the photograph she had had specially taken on her engagement, but he said he preferred the one in uniform. 'Though I'll have both if you like,' he had said, kissing her.

Easter wandered round the room; she looked out of the window on to the forlorn-looking, as yet unmade garden and beyond to where the fog hung amongst the bare trees, tattered and untidy, like gypsies' washing. She went to her own room, sitting down before her dressing-table and looking closely at her reflection. Her face showed little sign of the recent anguish. Always colourless, there were shadows under her eyes which gave them added depth. She put on some of the pale lipstick she had bought in Paris on their way back from the honeymoon. She picked up the photograph of York and, like her father-in-law some days previously, she studied it for a long time, as though she had never seen it before.

She went downstairs to the study and, taking a sheet of writing paper from the bureau, she wrote, 'Mavourneen', and then she paused, biting the end of her pencil. Presently she wrote, as a sub-heading: '*What I think I know about her.*'

(1) She was York's mistress for years. Months?
(2) York had broken with her, or so he believed, before the holiday in St Anton at which we met.
(3) York had certainly spent some time with her in Paris.
(4) She was older than he.
? She was Irish.
(5) When exchanging confidences about our 'pasts', there came a point when playfulness ended, beyond which York would not go.
(6) I think she was an actress. He always seemed knowledgeable about the stage and I do not know from what other source he could have picked up the odd scraps of information he sometimes produced.
(7) If I am right in thinking she was an actress this would account for the letters he received, from time to time, written, probably, from the provinces.
(8) I am almost certain that York saw her after we were married, though the letters did not say anything to confirm this, beyond asking him to meet her at 'the usual place'.
(9) I am almost certain that York gave her money.

Easter read through what she had written and, a few minutes later, she was again talking to her father-in-law on the telephone.

'I've been sorting out my thoughts about this woman,' she said. 'You said I might have that photograph back within the next day or so, but if I bring you the result of my thinking-back, could I have it?'

Jason hesitated. 'I've been sorting out things, too.'

'How do you mean?'

'I'll tell you when I see you. How about dining with me

here? I could send the car for you tomorrow evening.'

'Tomorrow? What about tonight?'

'I have an engagement.'

Easter said nothing in answer to this.

'Tomorrow, then?'

'All right.'

'And, Easter, dear. Is there a bobby outside the house now?'

'I don't know. The police car drives up from time to time.'

'You won't go out after dark, to a cinema or – or anything, will you?'

'There is nowhere I want to go, except to you tomorrow night. But we can't go on like this indefinitely. If anyone wants to do me any harm, they can easily wait until your police-protection is over.'

'By that time, please God, we shall have found the murderer.'

CHAPTER IX

It was unusual for the father, or indeed for any relative, of a murderee to ask to interview the doctor who conducted the post-mortem examination. But being who he was, Sir Jason Cragg's request was treated with respect. The Home Office pathologist himself was too busy, but he instructed his assistant to call on the bereaved father.

'Poor chap,' he said; 'if it makes him feel better to get himself into a bustle about his son's murder, it isn't for us to criticize him.'

So his young Chinese assistant called at Golden Fleece House in Throgmorton Street to be told that Sir Jason would see him at once.

'I want to ask you about my son's injuries, Doctor. I

understand you were present at the autopsy?'

'That is right, sir.'

'Will you tell me in your own words, not necessarily the words you used in your report, what sort of injuries these were?'

The young surgeon brought out his notebook in which he had made jottings. 'Altogether there were seven stab wounds in the back, sir. They were in varying depth and degrees of violence. It is not easy to say in which order they were inflicted, but it is obvious that the first blow must have been successful in penetrating the chest above the first rib, and thus causing your son to be unable to turn to defend himself. This first blow probably brought him down and made him unconscious. The lungs and kidneys were severely injured. The heart was untouched.'

'Could you penetrate as far as the heart from the back, with a long enough weapon?'

'With a long enough weapon, yes, provided the victim was thin. But your son . . .'

'Quite.' Sir Jason tapped his paper-knife on his desk with the regularity of a woodpecker.

'Five of the wounds were successful, sir. That is, they were penetrating, two were not.'

'You mean, they were surface wounds?'

'Not exactly. But they weren't mortal; he could have survived if he had only had these two.'

'Would you regard the whole picture as being a very savage attack indeed?'

'Very much so. The photographs which the police have taken, if I may say so, are very good. I mean, sir, they'll make a good show at the murder trial. They won't leave any doubt in the minds of the jury.'

'That there was malice aforethought and evil intent?'

'That the murderer certainly meant business. There is an excellent photograph taken as he lay, untouched, face down, half inside the cupboard. And then there are the photographs taken at the mortuary. Every member of the jury will have copies of those photographs before them for most of the trial; it will keep their minds on the job. The police have to go so carefully with the evidence, these days, they can let themselves go on the photographs.'

'Thanks, I don't want to see them,' Sir Jason said drily. 'Now, what about the weapon?'

'A very sharp knife.'

'The police have mentioned stilettos, daggers, jack-knives, double-edged knives.'

'It doesn't do any harm to generalize when the search for a knife, or weapon of any kind, is going on. A dagger is a dagger.' The young surgeon gave a very Eastern shrug. 'The only thing that is certain is that it was sharp, otherwise it would not have penetrated so far.'

'That would depend, surely, on the weight and strength behind the blow?'

'Oh, yes. And, if you have experience, it is easy to tell if a sharp knife was used.'

'I see; I'm just trying to reconstruct this horrible scene in my mind, Doctor. Let us say my son opened his wardrobe, presumably to take something out. He kneeled down to reach his case or something and, as he did so, he was attacked from the back. One violent blow and he would fall forward, in, probably, the position in which he was finally found. After the first blow the assailant had it all his own way, he could go on stabbing for as long as he liked?'

'He had it all his own way, as you say, from the first. It was a cowardly and brutal attack.'

'It must have been someone who hated my son very much to have gone on stabbing after the first damage was done.'

'It certainly was not someone who loved him,' the surgeon said, without the vestige of a smile.

'But isn't it mad to go on stabbing after it was unnecessary?'

'Isn't murder mad anyway?'

Sir Jason stirred restlessly in his chair. He had not yet brought himself to ask the question which burned him because he did not know how to make it light and casual enough.

'You think it could have been any sort of knife at all?'

'I didn't say that, sir,' the surgeon protested. 'There are a lot of knives it could not have been. But if you showed me a knife, I could say, roughly, whether that knife could have done it or not. The paper-knife that you are holding, for instance.'

'Well?'

'That could not have done it. I dare say you could kill someone with it if you found the right spot and put enough strength behind it, but it would make a more jagged wound, if you understand me.'

'Perfectly.' Sir Jason looked at the weapon in hand in some surprise. 'Well, thank you, Doctor, you have been most co-operative. I'm sorry to have bothered you.'

With the intention of sending him a case of sherry, he noted down the visitor's name and address and walked him to the door.

He cleared his throat nervously: 'You'd say, of course, that the assailant was roughly a man of my son's size?'

The little Chinese stopped and turned round. 'Not at all, not at all!' he protested in his thin high voice. 'Did I give you that impression? I am sorry. I could have done it, even I, if I had had a sharp enough knife.'

'A woman, perhaps, could have done it.' Sir Jason employed, in his agitation, a slightly macabre jocularity.

'Certainly a woman could have done it. Oh, but no!' the little yellow man added, shocked. 'No woman would perform such a violent act; once, perhaps, in anger, but seven times; I think not.'

'It is curious that a police surgeon could say that.'

'Only speaking non-professionally.' The Chinese was becoming confused. 'I did not mean from my experience professionally. From that I know that a woman can do everything, anything. A woman can be a monster. If you'll forgive me, sir, when you asked if a woman could have done the injuries to your son, I reacted personally, as it were. There are no unnatural women amongst my acquaintances, therefore I do not feel qualified to give an opinion.'

'Perhaps you have been lucky in your experience of women,' Sir Jason said wistfully. 'Thank you for coming, Doctor. Good day to you.'

One minute later he took the photograph out of his despatch-case and stared thoughtfully at it. 'Monster?'

The buzzer sounded at his side and, when he pressed the button, the husky, canned voice of his secretary, Miss Blockley, was heard saying: 'The representative of the Board of Trade to see you, Sir Jason.'

'Bring him in,' and wearily Sir Jason put away the photograph.

CHAPTER X

They dined at Scheherazade, a restaurant in the basement below the block of flats in which Sir Jason lived, and at which he was a frequent visitor. The decor was so exotic, the lighting so indefinite, and the atmosphere so unfresh, that one had the distinct feeling of being at the bottom of the sea, and a tropical sea at that. So oppressive was the environment that Easter had the feeling that she was a fish, incapable of crisp thought and inclined to open and shut her mouth without saying anything.

They ate pressed duck stuffed with *foie gras* and drank Château *Mouton Rothschild* and Jason observed unhappily that, though only nine days since his son's death, they were undoubtedly enjoying their meal. This, he comforted himself, was not indicative of the regard they had for York, but merely showed a healthy condition of their nerves.

During the meal he told Easter what provision he was making for her. Though York had had every intention of making a will, he had not done so at the time of his death. The amount of the company's shares, however, that he had possessed would bring in an income equal to the salary he had received from the firm during his lifetime. He was arranging to have the shares transferred to Easter. The house would be hers in any case, Sir Jason pointed out, as he had given it to them both on their marriage. He, Sir Jason, would be responsible for the death duties which they hoped might not be too high.

He patted Easter's hand and told her in a fatherly way that she had nothing to worry about. She could look round for another husband, he said magnanimously and, if she had any children, he would look after them as though they were his own.

Easter remained unenthusiastic about this proposal. She said gloomily that she was going to be just the job for some lazy twerp who wanted to be kept without having to do any work for the rest of his life.

They talked about the Ramsgates and Easter said she thought it might be nice to give John Ramsgate a sum of money as a present, as from York's will. 'They've been so kind to me and with two children they can use it,' Easter added thoughtfully. And Sir Jason patted her hand again and thought what a nice gal she was.

Relaxed, her cigarette smoke ascending in a straight line from between her fingers, Easter looked round her at the murals depicting scenes from the Arabian Nights.

'Scheherazade . . . what does it mean?'

'Don't you know? Scheherazade was the daughter of the Grand Vizier who married the King of Arabia whose habit it was to kill off each of his wives when he tired of them. When Scheherazade's time to be killed arrived she told the King a story every night, and, when she reached the most exciting part, said it would be continued in her next, that is the following evening, and thus she kept herself from being killed like the others. Clever, wasn't it? But all women are "tellers of tales", aren't they?'

'More so than men, do you think?'

'Much, much more.' Yes, he thought, 'Mavourneen' might be Scheherazade with her wild look and her fabulous mouth.

His brain was oddly divided; he appeared to be giving his whole attention to Easter and to what he had to tell her, but his eyes wandered to each woman in the restaurant and to everyone who entered or left. He could remember every small detail of The Photograph and, if he saw her again, he would know her instantly. As an ornament in the front of the coronet of hair, he remembered, she was wearing a Turkish-looking brooch, a crescent of brilliants holding an octagonal star. It was only a matter of time, part of him thought with a thrill of excitement, before they would meet. With his money, with the powers he had, the tracking-down of this woman could be completed. Would be.

'Let's go up to the flat,' Easter murmured. 'I can't remember what I've come for; I feel like a fish.'

'You've eaten too much, dear.'

'No, it's not that. Everyone looks like a fish, look how slowly they are moving . . .'

'It must be the claret.' Sir Jason signed the bill and they rose.

Everyone watched the good-looking couple leave; some nudged one another and whispered: 'Sir Jason Cragg, you know, whose son . . .' There were a few unkind and furtive smiles. 'That's his daughter-in-law, the widow . . .'

In his flat Easter drew aside the curtains and looked down over the wet slate roofs while Sir Jason fiddled about with the grog tray. 'This should be called the Eagle's Nest!' she said. 'High up above the streets of London.'

'Easter, *dear*, we were fish a minute ago. In any case I'm not a bit like an eagle, much more like a whale. Moby Dick, the great white whale. Armagnac?' He handed her a moderately-sized globe-shaped glass.

Easter laughed. 'Yes, perhaps you are like Moby Dick, but please, the real one and not the plastic one working by remote control that we saw in the film.' She sipped her brandy dreamily. 'Besides,' she murmured, 'Moby Dick had little piggy, knowing eyes.'

'Perhaps I've little piggy, knowing eyes.' Sir Jason looked anxiously at himself in the looking-glass.

'You haven't, darling, and you've the mind of an eagle, anyway.' Through the glass he could see the shining top of Easter's head as she looked down into her drink. The thin man was wildly crying for help: 'Help, Help!' but the voice was not of this world, it was higher than the cry of a bat and there was no one to hear.

Easter sang in a cracked, soft little voice:

> 'You're the cream in my coffee,
> You're the salt in my stew
> You will always be
> My necessity
> I'd be lost without you.'

Enchanted, he cried: 'But that was long before your time!'

'I was just a little bundle,' she murmured, 'wrapped in the *News of the World.*'

'Not even that! That song was a favourite in nineteen twenty something!'

'It's true, though,' Easter said, looking straight at him with her calm eyes.

Sir Jason lowered himself into his big wing chair as gingerly as though he were a bubble that he wanted to keep intact; he felt, in fact, rather like a bubble. But not for long. It is bad for a bubble to be sat on and no sooner had he sat down, his brandy on a small table at his side, than Easter sat on his knee.

He was shocked, of course, but you can be shocked and other things at the same time, and the pleasure he felt greatly exceeded any other feeling and that went for the shock, too.

There was no deep emotion in it because the thin man would have had to share in that and he, alas, had vanished. Jason felt exactly the same pleasure as he had felt at the times when his nurse tickled him as a small boy. It was all too degrading to stand thinking about; he abandoned thought and simply went on feeling delightful and when, finally, she slipped to the floor, they were both giggling like schoolchildren.

'That's the trouble,' Easter said, continuing to sit where she was, between his knees, and sipping her brandy. 'You've never been young. You married ridiculously early, before you could have any fun, and then you were left with a baby boy and all the cares in the world on your great hefty shoulders. And that is what was wrong with York; he, on the other hand, never grew up because *you* kept all his troubles, or nearly all. He never had to make his way in the world, build up a flourishing business and all the things you've done. He was born with a silver spoon in his mouth, as they say, and he was spoon-fed right up to the day he died!'

Nine nights ago, the thin man might have reminded them, had he not been in abeyance.

'There was always you between York and the hard cold world and so he never developed properly. In spite of being a huge man, he was a shadow, really. That is why he never dealt properly with . . . with this "Mavourneen". You wouldn't have treated her the way he did.'

'How do you know how he treated her?'

'One can only guess,' Easter shrugged. 'It is clear that

whatever way he treated her was the wrong way, isn't it?'

'You mean, if she killed him?'

'Yes, if she killed him. He must have bungled the affair horribly. Getting killed was a proof of failure, poor darling,' she added. After a pause she went on: 'He mucked things up, didn't he?'

'I don't think I want to talk about York, God rest his soul,' Sir Jason said.

'We'll talk about you, and how young you feel,' Easter smiled up at him. 'Shall we, Jason? Shall we?'

Presently the buzzer went to tell them that the car was waiting and, as he carefully wrapped Easter in her mink coat:

'Take good care of yourself,' he sang,
'You belong to me.'

'Thank you for the lovely evening,' Easter whispered, holding up her face to be kissed. 'I suppose it is naughty of us, but it's been quite a party!'

He held her small face between his hands: 'Does it say anything in the prayer-book about not marrying your daughter-in-law?'

'The prayer-book doesn't say anything, I'm sure,' she answered lightly, 'but everyone else would, at the moment, anyway. You see now, darling, what I meant about me not coming to live here with you?'

'I see now,' he murmured dreamily, 'and I'm going to kiss you.'

The buzzer went again.

Easter said: 'Oh, bother. I really came to tell you things I've got written down here on a paper in my handbag.'

'Never mind about that now.'

'Jason, I must go.'

'Yes, darling Easter, I suppose you must.'

'That photograph?'

'What?'
'The photograph, darling.'
'Easter, I can't let you go.'
'Please, the photograph. Is it there, in your case?'
Holding it, she threw her arms round his neck and kissed him. She ran out, slamming the gates of the lift and blowing him a kiss through the iron grille.

As Sir Jason moved about his flat, preparing for bed, he was still using the old consolation: 'It hasn't happened.'

CHAPTER XI

It was easy not to see Easter for the next eight days. He had a great deal of work to do and the need for an urgent visit to Amsterdam occurred. He asked his secretary to telephone to his daughter-in-law to tell her that he had to leave the country for a couple of nights and to ask if there was anything she wanted.

On his return he spoke to her himself. She asked him to dinner with her and, as it happened, the best evening for him was the one following his return.

'That would do,' Easter said, 'except that I'm having my hair done in Dover Street at four.'

But there was no other evening available in the near future, so it was decided that Easter would leave dinner prepared, come to town and have her hair done, go to Throgmorton Street in a taxi and drive down to Putney with Sir Jason. This being one of the occasions when it was simpler not to use the chauffeur, Sir Jason would drive himself.

At the appointed time Easter arrived at Golden Fleece House. She sat in the luxurious waiting-room for a bare five minutes before being joined by Sir Jason. He apologized for keeping her waiting and asked if she would mind walking round to the car park with him, or whether she would prefer to wait until he got the car. It was a fine frosty evening and Easter said she would walk round with him. They left the impressive entrance, with its great bronze doors not yet shut for the night, the commissionaire saluting them as they passed.

It was a small square enclosure, almost pitch dark, a well between the immensely high walls of two new blocks of offices.

'I can't see a thing,' Easter complained, wondering at the roughness underfoot.

'Wait a minute – stay where you are until I turn on the lights.'

When the quiet little cul de sac was illuminated, Easter could see that there was barely room for the parking of three large cars.

'That's the back of Golden Fleece House,' Sir Jason pointed. 'Hop in. When they were rebuilding, this small enclosure was left because of an Ancient Lights rule, something to do with that building, which, by the way, they are going to pull down. It's a small fur factory, almost derelict. Two others and myself pay a small annual sum for the use of this little space, but when we have to give it up, it's going to be a nuisance.'

They slid out into the bustle of the city's rush hour.

Sir Jason's old Rolls-Royce was a 40/50 drop-head coupé with a body specially built for him twenty-five years ago by Hooper.

'I'd love to drive it some time,' Easter said wistfully.

'You can drive it now,' Sir Jason said promptly.

'Better not, there's too much traffic and I don't really know my way about the City.'

'Talking of cars,' Sir Jason said, 'what about York's Bentley, Easter?'

'It's in the garage. I've had no occasion to use it; it is such a nuisance trying to find somewhere to park that

I find it is easier to come up to town by train.'

'You're not going to want to keep it?'

'Definitely not,' Easter said promptly.

'Well, I'll tell you what I've had in mind. I know I can get a good price for you if you let me sell the Bentley within the next month or so. And I propose giving you a little runabout.'

'I would like that,' Easter nodded enthusiastically, 'something small that I can take into Harrods under my arm, or nearly.'

'That sort of thing. An MG perhaps. And I'd like to give it to you; I was going to give you one, as it happens, for your birthday, that is some time in March, isn't it? Right, I'll see to that. And if you really want to drive this, you can drive me down to Southampton on Sunday.' He mentioned some friends in the shipping world, who lived on the edge of the New Forest and with whom he was going to lunch. The trip would be fun, he said, if Easter would come with him, and so it was arranged; he would call for Easter and she could drive all the way, if she liked.

They glided out through the suburbs, taking a complicated route but one which Sir Jason was convinced was shorter, through Walham Green and Parson's Green, and finally, over Putney Bridge and home.

Easter's house was reached through the gateposts of what had once been the approach to a mansion. Four modern houses of luxurious type had been built in the space available. Though close together, they were cleverly arranged to give the impression of isolation. Big banks of rhododendrons and azaleas had been left separating the houses; the gardens had, in fact, been as little disturbed as was feasible. Each house had its own gravel approach and garage and yet was hidden from the others by pre-existing screens of evergreen.

Easter's house looked out across a small space which was to be planted as a lawn, over banks of dark-leaved rhododendrons to the bare trees beyond. There was, as yet, no independent lighting in the small estate, though the installation of lighting for the drives was under discussion with the local council. Each house was responsible for the lighting of its own drive and approach.

As there was no one at home, the house and garden were in darkness and the headlights of the car swung round, lighting up every corner.

'It's a damned awful house for you to be in alone,' Jason grumbled. 'The police may be giving you special protection but I can't see how it can be adequate. Anyone could lie concealed in those bloody great bushes.'

'I don't feel like that about it,' Easter told him. 'I'm not more than fifty yards from the next house; look, that red glow is their kitchen window, with a red blind. I've only got to give a small scream and the people in all three houses could hear me. And that new block of flats positively overlooks the back of the house; if I gave a shout there would be a head out of every window, in no time. As it is, people spend ages simply staring out of their windows, down on to us, from the new flats. And as for the police protection, I hear the car crunching up three or four times during the night. I don't think there's a man there all the time now, there would be no point in it; anyone who wanted to break in would know all about a watchman by now.'

But Sir Jason was not happy. Whilst Easter made the final preparations for their meal he sat gloomily drinking his son's sherry under no illusion that this particular evening was going to be a happy one.

They dined at a low table beside the fire in the sitting-room. Candles lit the table and the fire burned brightly.

During dinner he told Easter that he was sorry, but he must talk about the police and their investigations for a moment. 'I'm not going to bother you,' he said, 'but you ought to know how things are going.'

'Going? Are they going at all?'

'Of course. But I haven't let them bother you. I think you told them all they wanted to know. Anything else they've had to come to me for. You said you'd been making notes, or something, about that gal. What was it you had to tell me that night at Scheherazade?'

'It was about the mysterious Mavourneen. I tried to remember every little thing, in the light of my having found the photograph, that would tell me something about her. After I had finished and read it over, it looked as though I might have got something. But with the passage of time ... I don't know. There's awfully little to go on.'

'It doesn't matter a bit about the passage of time, as you call it. I'm a ruthless man, Easter. I know you think I'm an old dear, but I'm not. I wouldn't have got where I am if I'd been a woolly-minded-dodo.'

Easter leaned across the table and put a cool hand on his.

'Don't get cross. And please try to see the thing from my point of view. I've told you how I feel about it, our private life dragged in the gutter. I'd much prefer, at this stage, to let the whole thing lie!'

'And the murderer of my son go ... scot free?'

Easter shrugged.

'Or live to do it again? Show me the notes you made.'

Easter did so and he read them through carefully. 'May I take these with me?'

'To show the police?' she asked quickly.

'To brood over.'

'All right.' Easter rested her head on her hand, her newly-set hair falling forward, hiding her face.

'It's no good,' he said, after a long pause, 'I'm not comfortable in this damned house. And I don't know how you could be. I'll be only too happy the day you decide to move out finally. When is that going to be?'

'It depends on a lot of things ...'

It may be that the atmosphere of the house was strangely oppressive, or it may be that their own minds pictured over-vividly the scene of York's death; whatever it was, it was quite clear that they could not get back to the happy relationship of the dinner they had last had together.

'Don't let's talk about the police and whatever investigations they may be making. Nothing they can do will bring York back. You say you're a ruthless man; by that do you mean you're lacking in pity? Short of kindness? Because you aren't either of those things.'

'I mean that when I say I'm going to do a thing, I generally do it. I don't let things stand in my way; I don't let sentiment clog the wheels.'

'Don't you?' Easter was silent, thinking it over. 'I don't either. Maybe I'm ruthless, too. But as I see it now, with the first horror and pity worn off, it might be that what happened was all for the best. Yes, you're shocked. You can be ruthless, but you don't like me to be. But let's face it, Jason: York's life came to a sudden end, he had no pain. If he had lived, there might have been a great deal of pain and unhappiness, because how could our marriage have stood up to the years?'

'Don't! I will not talk that way, or even allow myself to think that way. I loved York; you think I loved him too much, ruined him. Well, perhaps I did. But this I am decided about. I'm not going to let whoever killed him get away with it. I'm repeating that to you, Easter, to let you know I feel the same about it as I did at first. Now, I won't discuss it any more; I can see you'd rather not. I'm going and leaving you in this godforsaken house only under the strongest protest, as I've said before. Repeat, strongest protest.'

'All right,' Easter murmured. 'But I'm not too worried about the Mavourneen person. A woman couldn't have done that frightful damage.'

'You're wrong there. I'm satisfied that a woman could have done it. An angry woman, a wronged woman, as they say. You won't remember the old song with the line in it:

"He was her man, he done her wrong." It's gone through my head often since I saw that photograph.'

' "He was her man, he done her wrong." ' Easter's arms were crossed and she rocked slightly to and fro in her chair as she repeated it. 'Yes, could be. But she would have got another man to do the dirty for her.'

'Very far-fetched indeed,' Sir Jason snapped. ' "He was my man, he done me wrong," so you go and stab him to death for me? Don't be silly!'

'It was far-fetched that York was stabbed to death at all,' she argued.

The evening was not being a success, but how could it be?

Jason and Easter, Easter and Jason; he felt that it was no easy matter to slip out of the old relationship and into the new. 'I always wanted a daughter,' he remembered saying when York first presented his fiancée, and the curious situation that had developed made him feel vaguely incestuous, uncomfortably like the Dirty Old Man of debutantes' gossip. In the circumstances of everyday life it was not easy to change the habit of his regard for Easter.

He sat beside the cheerful fire, sipping his brandy and feeling a deep melancholy. Easter sat on the floor; she was wearing a red woollen dressing-gown affair, which she called a house coat, with a long satin collar and cuffs and, with her hands clasped round her knees, she leaned against him slightly. She looked oddly childlike and charming.

'*Deep-bosomed daughter of the ocean*,' Jason thought, and it was not Easter to whom his thoughts referred.

'You're a business-like little thing, aren't you?' he said dispassionately. 'I mean – this document you've just handed to me – were you quietly thinking all these things over to yourself all the time you were married to York?'

'Don't you think most women are always quietly on the look out for unfaithfulness in their husbands?'

'Do I? I dunno.' He laughed shortly. 'But I do know that,

if I were in any doubt as to whether you had really loved York, this indictment, as you might call it, wouldn't leave me in any doubt.'

Easter seemed surprised. 'But it depends what you mean by love. There is affection which you could call love.'

'It sounds trite, I suppose you'll say you felt affection for York,' he returned irritably, 'and that was as far as it went! I don't know the first thing about women; don't understand the species. There's a load of mischief here.' He tapped the pocket into which he had put Easter's memo. 'You've used a good bit of imagination, too. Such odd things you've remembered! And there's nothing really helpful, nothing that's going to help us to trace her,' he grumbled. 'Pure guesswork. And how do you know she was Irish? The name? It doesn't follow at all. And why did you want the photograph back?'

She put a hand on his knee. 'Aren't you being a bit unfair? The photograph was York's most treasured possession; he evidently couldn't bring himself to destroy it. It seems a mean thing to bandy about something a dead man thought a lot of and wanted kept secret.'

'Average decent behaviour flies out of the window when murder comes in at the door.'

And, rather pleased with the phrase, he prepared to leave.

'Be sure you lock yourself in properly,' he told her. 'Promise me you won't forget?' And, giving her a hasty peck, he hurried away.

Unkissed Easter stood a minute, forlorn, in her brightly lit hall. There was not a sound, not even a clock ticked. Not a gurgle came from the perfectly-run central heating. Not a breath of wind stirred the stiff, brittle leaves of the rhododendrons in the drive.

It was the house, Sir Jason decided as he drove back to town. The house gave him the heebie jeebies; it was not possible to have a repetition of their happy evening of the previous week in a house which had known such violent happenings. He felt that the house, with its smooth perfection, was in league with the murderer against him. Through that sleek hall the killer had crept, he had stepped across the thick, cream-coloured rugs on the hall parquet, up the bare polished oak stair, past the deep window-recess filled with indoor plants and the thick interlined pale gold curtains of the landing. He, Jason, would not care to spend a night alone in that house and it irritated him that his daughter-in-law should be insensitive to its ambience.

It provoked him, too, that he and Easter did not agree in regard to what must be done about the photograph. It piqued him not to be able to discuss with her what exactly he intended to do about it; he had deliberately said that he did not let sentiment clog the wheels, with the idea of letting her know that he thought *she* did. But she hadn't seen it that way; she had retaliated by telling him that she, too, was ruthless. Of all the absurdities!

CHAPTER XII

In the gentlemen's cloakroom of the Piccadilly Hotel, Sir Jason put on his almost black sunglasses and peered anxiously at himself. It was a dull winter's day, with a sullen fog hanging over London; no day for sunglasses. Nor, Sir Jason observed, were the dark glasses in any way a disguise. They gave him, however, a confidence he needed. Behind them he felt more secure; he could pass an acquaintance without it appearing obvious that he had seen them and wished to pass unnoticed. No amount of disguise could, in fact, have concealed his identity. His figure was both distinguished and distinctive and he had a particularly individual way of walking, a bustling, sprightly walk; for a heavy man, he was singularly light on his feet.

Taking a last anxious look, Sir Jason wished himself luck,

picked up his despatch-case, hurried up the stairs and out on to the crowded pavements. Taking his bearings, he steered north-north-east, straight into darkest Soho. He found the shop he had in mind exactly where he had expected to find it. The window was filled with shiny photographs. He went inside. The shop was empty but an assistant came out at once from behind a curtain at the back of the counter. Sir Jason felt unable to see any more of him than his moustache which was of an unusual kind, being waxed at the ends and moulded into a form that strongly resembled the handlebars of a racing bicycle.

'Er . . .' Sir Jason fumbled inside his despatch-case. 'I wonder if you could help me? Could you shed any light on this photograph?'

'You want to know who it is, or what? Is it one of ours?' The young man held it up to the light. 'No, it's not one of ours.'

'It's a copy, taken from a photograph that might, originally, have been one of yours. I had it done from the original at Harrods.'

'Got the original?'

'Unfortunately not.'

'We've got hundreds and hundreds of this sort of photograph. Tin files packed with them out the back.'

'I realize that it must be so, but what about that file or reference number in white in the left-hand corner?' Sir Jason knew it by heart. 'C.L. 1007. Ser.L.17.'

The young man shook his moustache and his head behind it slowly from side to side. 'It's not ours. It's like a laundry mark, see, sir? Could be any photographer.'

'I've never seen a photograph with the serial or file number, or whatever you call it, on the front,' Sir Jason protested, heartened by the 'sir'.

'Oh well . . .' the young man paused for the suitable words and then leaned confidentially across the counter. 'It's a publicity photograph, this is; taken for a theatrical agent or some such. On this type of photograph you often find the serial mark; it's nearly always used by this class of photographer.'

'Ah!' Sir Jason felt happily that he was really getting somewhere. 'I see.'

Co-operative to a degree, the young man flashed out a dozen or so photographs of a similar type: 'That's our "laundry mark",' he said whimsically.

'Are there many of you?'

'This class of photographer? Coo, yes! Half a hundred in this district, shouldn't wonder.'

'In this district? But perhaps this photograph wasn't taken in this district. It might not have been taken in London at all. It could have been taken in the provinces, on the Continent, South Africa, America, anywhere.'

The young man was thoughtfully studying the photograph. 'In that case,' he remarked, 'you've got your work cut out if you want to find out who this dame is. But it looks to me . . .' he said slowly.

'Yes?'

'It looks to me like this is a West End job. Could be wrong. Could be USA, as you suggest. Could be. But it's worth trying, if you're all that keen.'

'Worth trying the other half-hundred, you mean?'

The young man nodded, handing the photograph back to Sir Jason with all the sympathy and understanding in the world in his warm look. 'I suppose I can't tempt you with anything else?'

'You could,' Sir Jason stated, 'but, as you say, I've got my work cut out. And I've no doubt you can use this.' He leaned across the counter and shook hands with the young man.

This . . . was a pound note.

Sir Jason took a taxi-cab in a north-north-westerly direction. A firm trading under the name of Any Questions Ltd. occupied rooms in a large house in Harley Street and existed for the purpose of answering any enquiries that might be put to them. The minimum charge was half a guinea for a simple question like: 'Where can I find the Velasquez picture, "The Water-Seller of Seville"?' and rose in proportion to the amount of work involved in finding the answer. It was their proud boast that, unless a question were leading or rhetorical, in which case it was disqualified, they never failed to find the answer.

Though they covered a wide field, they did not, of course, include personal questions. Sir Jason could not, for instance, produce the photograph, ask 'Who is this?' and expect to be told. But what he was able to do was to ask them to make a list for him of all the photographers in the West End of London who took photographs 'like this' with the file number in the left-hand corner written in tiny figures.

'Yes, sir,' the young lady said briskly, pen poised ready to take down his particulars. 'Your name and address, please?'

'I'll call in.'

She looked doubtful. 'I don't know how long it will take.'

'It's very urgent.'

'Yes, I'm sure it is. I'll see what we can do.'

At the same time two days later Sir Jason was standing in the same place with the coveted list in his hand. There were twenty-two names and addresses, not half a hundred. Twenty-two. He smiled at the young lady. 'Thank you very much indeed,' he said cordially. 'And now I think you can help me some more. Can you give me the address of an investigation agent who could go round to all these photographers and find out which one uses this particular type of identification mark?'

The young lady's eyebrows shot up. 'You mean a private detective?'

Sir Jason looked uncomfortable. 'Well, not really.'

But that, of course, was what he did mean and before

long he was speeding down Harley Street. But not more than a block and a half; the private detective also had an address in Harley Street. On either side of his lair, citadels of medical respectability stood, still unstormed. But in a steamy attic, in the upper air of Harley Street, the investigator sat, like a spider, and sent out busy little men all over London, spying, creeping, peering, asking, peeping, and then sending in enormous bills to his clients: 'For Services Rendered'.

This particular commission was simple but expensive. It was a matter of the men's time but, realizing almost at once that in this case the expenditure of money would be no objection, he became enthusiastic. Sir Jason left three copies of the photograph behind so that three men might function at the same time. He also left a large deposit in the form of five-pound notes as a security, arising from the fact that he did not wish to leave his name, address or telephone number. He arranged to return in three days' time and, when the three days were up, he had the name and address of the photographer where the original photograph had been taken. He paid the remainder of his bill most gratefully and was uncomfortably aware, as he slipped the three photographs back into his despatch-case, that his hands were trembling conspicuously.

Sir Jason felt almost homesick for the sympathetic young man with the odd moustache as he entered the new photographer's, which was not half a mile from the original shop.

This time everything was brisk and impersonal. He was attended to by a blonde whose mind was clearly not on her job. The photograph was taken, she said, last February, nearly a year ago. She supposed that if he wanted the address of the customer, there was no objection, but it was unusual, very. The look she gave him was inclined to be saucy, but as Sir Jason's eyes were hidden from her behind his glasses she was not sure of herself. The production of the wallet and the pound note brought her to the alert more quickly than anything.

Within a remarkably short time Sir Jason had the paper, with a name and address written on it, clutched in his hand and was hurrying down the street. He felt almost dizzy with excitement and went into a coffee bar which he happened to be passing. He sipped a *cappuccino* and smoked a cigarette before he felt calm enough to read what was written on the paper:

> Mrs Valentine Millage
> Rosedale,
> Victory Avenue,
> Edgware, Middlesex.

How relentlessly disappointing!

'Mrs Valentine Millage' didn't even tell him whether Valentine was her own name or that of her husband. 'Rosedale, Victory Avenue, Edgware.' Perhaps she had two little 'kiddiz'. If that was so, how dared she look like that?

Almost furtively Sir Jason slid one of the photographic copies out of his despatch-case and studied it.

'A "Messalina of the Suburbs",' he decided, with a heavy sigh, and ordered himself another *cappuccino*.

CHAPTER XIII

Much travelled though he was, Sir Jason made a journey he had never yet undertaken; he took the Underground to Edgware. He did not even know until now that beyond Hampstead the train took an upward slope, emerged into the open air and ran along an embankment some feet above the houses and gardens for several miles. Arriving at his destination, he emerged from the station feeling as conspicuous and uncertain of himself as a camel on the shores of Loch Lomond. There was no taxi-rank that he could see, nor was there a policeman of whom he could ask the way. There was, however, a road sweeper with a friendly eye who was able to send him in the right direction.

It was a long walk. Sir Jason was wearing his black topcoat, his Lock's bowler hat, a Paisley-patterned scarf in blue and red silk, and carried a beautifully furled umbrella. He looked like someone who was in Edgware on a special mission. There seemed to be no other men walking the tree-lined roads; he met a great many women, some carrying shopping baskets and others wheeling prams. It was a dark and sullen-looking day, damp and raw, and as he tramped along he began to feel the utmost depression.

He passed a row of shops and an Odeon cinema where he again asked the way. He pressed on along a road of similar houses which petered out and the road looked as though it might be going out into the country, but it led simply past a sewage farm and a filling station, up a slight slope and on to a double-track by-pass road.

What a fool he had been, he thought. What idiotic streak of quixotry had directed him to make these personal investigations into his son's secrets? This was a job for the police, not for a middle-aged businessman; this was a sentimental journey, based on emotion rather than on common sense. It was instigated mainly by his desire not to have his son appear a fool, or worse, but also, and here he must be frank with himself, also because something about the face of the woman in the photograph compelled him to seek her out before, as he liked to put it this time, 'throwing her to the wolves'.

He trudged along wishing very much he was not on a by-pass; anyone in one of the cars zipping past might recognize him. Someone might stop to ask if they could give him a lift and he would have to pretend that his car had broken down, for what other excuse could he possibly make for being found where he was? It began to drizzle; he pressed on. He did not think of opening his umbrella; it had, in fact, never been opened. He passed a square concrete toffee-factory, whitewashed and tidy, and another filling station. Another row of shops. And then quite suddenly, out of the murk, he saw the words: 'Victory Avenue'.

Avondale, Ivycroft, Fernbank, The Lilacs, Wenlock. 'Victory' evidently referred to the 1918 Victory rather than the more recent one; the houses were thirty years old and more; they were semi-detached and had small front gardens.

Rosecroft and Rosedale were joined, like Siamese twins, and approached by a single pathway which divided, one branching to the door of Rosedale and the other to the front door of Rosecroft.

He pressed the bell of Rosedale which buzzed angrily like a live thing immediately under his finger. He did not feel the least excitement such as he had felt in the coffee bar. The long dreary walk from the station had successfully quelled any anticipatory thrills and the cries as from innumerable children from within only confirmed his apprehensions.

She was as black as his own Lock's bowler hat and a great deal more shiny. She held a baby in her arms and three small round-eyed toddlers peeped round her skirts; no doubt, Jason thought, there were others concealed beneath her skirts.

He raised his hat and said absurdly: 'Mrs Valentine Millage?' because, of course, he knew perfectly well it was not she. Out of the *chile con carne* of words that she broke into, he was just able to make out that Mrs Millage no longer lived here, and he was turning away, a broken man, when a brisk voice hailed him from the front downstairs window of Rosecroft.

'Bye bye!' The piccaninnies were shouting and waving their small black hands at him. Jason shut his eyes; soon he would wake up and tell Miss Blockley of the absurdities of his dream and they would laugh together about it.

'If you're looking for the Millages I might be able to help you.' The woman from Rosecroft leaned out of the window. She was a tortoiseshell cat of a woman, with thin lips and yellow eyes, but she had a pleasant enough expression on her face; at the moment, in fact, it was illuminated by something approaching delight.

'Do come in.' She ran out to the front door and was ushering Jason inside out of the rain before he was quite aware of it. But once inside he stood firm, refusing to have his umbrella taken from him, and deliberately refraining from removing his gloves. In the dim recesses at the back of his mind lurked the thought that the job of salesman to lonely-hearts in the outer suburbs was not without its compensations, but he suppressed it for further investigation at a more suitable moment.

Now what he must do was to extract all the information about the Millages that he could from Mrs Rosecroft, giving none whatever in return.

Out of a great deal of irrelevant detail, he was able to collect the salient facts: the Millages had lived for two years at Rosedale; Millage worked as a clerk at a well-known firm of instrument makers on the Great North Road; he was younger than Mrs Millage, who had 'been on the stage'. They were not happily married; Mrs Millage was 'flighty'; the ménage broke up, Mr Millage going home to his mother and Mrs Millage 'back to the stage'. (There were no children.) The house had been let to West Indians since last August.

It could fit in, Jason thought, trying hard to make it so. Nothing had turned out to expectation but *it could fit.*

'Was her name Mavourneen?' he asked.

The woman shook her head. 'Not that I know of, though it might have been her stage name. Val, he always called her. He was fond of her, mark you, and between ourselves, she treated him like dirt.'

She would. Yes, that was Mavourneen!

'I don't know how he put up with it,' the ginger-cat woman chatted on. 'But one day the worm turned; he flung her out.'

Or did she fling him?

'And no one's heard a word from her from that day to this.'

Hadn't they? Jason hugged himself mentally, happy again.

'I saw Ernest Millage only a fortnight ago walking along, on Watford by-pass. My hubby had a word with him, but nothink was said about Val.'

'You know Mr Millage's address, perhaps?'

She shook her head. 'No, but he's in the same job, that I do know.'

Jason jotted the name of the firm down in his notebook.

'Do let me make you a cup of tea, Mr – er – ?'

'You've been very kind.' Jason was at his most charming. He bowed slightly over her hand in a thoughtful way, as though he might kiss it in the Continental manner.

'You've had a long walk from the station!' But Jason was not to be drawn. Unctuously, he withdrew from the little house, giving nothing, not even a pound note, but leaving Mrs Rosecroft with the feeling that she had had an exciting day.

He knew that she and Mrs Rosedale, all the piccaninnies and a number of neighbours were watching his withdrawal. Aware that it would never again achieve its furled perfection, he opened his umbrella. The way back to the station seemed to take less than half the time. He was trying to make up his mind what would be the best reason he could give to the husband for his enquiries as to the whereabouts of his errant wife. The most fanciful, but the one he liked best, was that of himself as talent-spotter, but he was sadly aware that the one which would occur to the husband would be the obvious one, that he was a 'sugar-daddy'.

He decided finally that he would call at the factory and

ask to speak to Mr Millage on a matter of urgent business. In these circumstances the husband would be taken by surprise and would be less likely to dwell on detail than if he were to call at his home address. Sir Jason could state briefly that he was a solicitor and unable to give any reason, for the present, as to why he wanted the wife's address. Ten to one, the husband would give it immediately.

One 'prop', Sir Jason realized, that he must have, was his car.

Miss Blockley had no idea where he really was; he had made a variety of excuses for his recent absences from work; today it was Kempton Park races. His car was in the basement garage in Arlington Street; he could take it out, drive to the factory, and return to the city for an hour or two's work before evening.

He went back in the Underground to Leicester Square and had a snack luncheon at Fortnum and Mason's. He felt faintly unhappy about his deception of his faithful Miss Blockley. She had been so kind and understanding about his frivolous activities in the past few days. She knew how much work he had to do but she had smiled with the utmost forbearance when he had told her that he was going to Kempton Park. He knew that when he returned to the office at teatime she would ask how he had 'got on' and he would invent some picturesque lie about what he had lost or won.

It was curious, Sir Jason mused as he drove north, what a difference arriving at the factory on the Great North Road in his car would make to him. This afternoon he was a different being from the camel-like creature emerging from Edgware Station. He blew a great blast on the horn, which sent pedestrians scampering before him, almost flattered to be scattered by such a magnificent car.

CHAPTER XIV

Something, clearly, had to be done about the garden. Easter tied her hair up in a pretty yellow scarf, put on an old waterproof and went out to dig. It was drizzling dismally but she dug like a busy beaver, plunging the fork deeper into the soil with her foot on the tines as she had seen gardeners do. Presently she was sniffing frequently and was often obliged to remove a drop from the end of her nose with her pocket handkerchief, but her cheeks were a pretty pink and she felt delightfully healthy. The digging was no light work; the soil was heavy with moisture and the police had tramped it down hard, but she toiled happily all afternoon. The light was going when she finished the wide strip of soil they had planned to plant as an herbaceous border. She went round to the drying yard at the back and scraped the mud off her gumboots at the back door. As she was doing so the telephone rang.

'Is that you, Easter?' Jason's voice was high with excitement.

'Where are you talking from?'

'From the office, but on my private line. Can you hear me?'

Jason wanted to talk to her, could she possibly come up to town now, if he sent the car for her.

'What is it about, darling?' Easter asked.

Jason, choosing his words carefully so that they would not be understood by any chance listener, told her that he had been making certain enquiries; she might be able to guess in what direction.

She was quite wordless; shocked into silence.

He had been more successful than would have been thought possible. 'Are you still there?'

'Yes, yes, I'm here.'

'You're so quiet.'

She ran a tired hand across her forehead.

'I've done nothing that you didn't want me to do. With regard to the police, I mean. I've been very, very discreet.' There was a touch of pride in his voice. 'But I must discuss with you what we are going to tell the police, in the light of what I have discovered.'

'But, darling,' Easter protested. 'You couldn't do much without the photograph.'

'Couldn't I? I could have copies made of it.'

'But that was mean!' she cried.

'You won't think so when you hear what I've found out. But we must get on with things, Easter, and I must talk to you quick.'

'I'm far too tired to be intelligent about anything tonight,' she said. 'Wouldn't tomorrow do?'

'I thought if you could come now . . . But I won't press it, dear. I'm dining with a friend at the club; fellow just home from the Middle East; haven't seen him for a couple of years; I wouldn't be happy about putting him off.'

'Wait a minute.' She sounded tired, as, indeed, she suddenly was. 'I'm coming up to town to have my hair done tomorrow, and then I planned to have lunch and go to a movie with Jill Ramsgate. I could come to you after that.'

'You mean, spend the evening together?'

'Here.'

'There? Why not Arlington Street?'

'I don't like coming back home late alone, and I don't want to drag you out at that time of night. Do come here! We might meet in town and drive down together. I'll order some smoked salmon to be sent and we'll have dinner here, by the fire. How's that? I'll leave everything ready so it won't be any trouble.'

'All right, if you prefer it that way.'

'And, Jason . . . you won't do anything more until we've

talked it over, will you, about the police or anything? I'm a bit frightened. You've been barging about doing I don't know what. And we don't know what we're up against. I don't like it.'

'I don't like it either. Are you really frightened, Easter?'

'Only in a way. I'm frightened for you. I'm afraid you've been stirring things up.'

'I did warn you. And I'm not going to let you persuade me to drop this thing; we're on to something, I'm sure, and with every day that passes the clues are getting cold, as they say.'

'What time shall we meet?'

'What time does your cinema end?'

'I'm not sure. Jill is staying up in town; she and John are dining with friends.'

'Should we say six, then?'

'Yes, that would do nicely. What about meeting at Green Park Station and if you were held up I could shelter under the Ritz arches.'

'I can't wait long at Green Park Station; it's a bus stop.'

'Just by the Ritz main entrance, then? I won't keep you waiting, promise. I'll be there in good time.'

'Right. I wish I could see you now, Easter, all the same. For God's sake, see the house is properly locked up, and don't hang about in the back yard in the dark, or anything.'

'No, I won't. Promise, again. But do let me remind you; there are burglar catches on all the windows and double locks on the front and back doors. So don't worry. It's you I'm worried about.'

'Hum. Well, see you tomorrow night.'

'Good night –' Easter gently replaced the receiver – 'darling,' she whispered, her eyes shining.

CHAPTER XV

One can feel as exposed to the weather in the streets of London as on some Lancashire pike. As he left the little sheltered corner in which he parked his car and turned into the street, an icy-cruel wind threw itself against Jason and caused him to clutch his hat and bend forward with watering eyes. The sky lay, heavily grey, on the rooftops of the city. There's snow on the way, Jason thought; I must ring up Easter and tell her to stay at home.

But sitting in his warm office he changed his mind. He must let the poor kid have her outing if she wanted, however simple it might be. It would do her good to get away from that house even for an afternoon.

He lunched at the Savoy with two business friends and as he took a taxi back to the city he noticed that the weather had not improved, though it was still not snowing. At half past five he asked Miss Blockley for his letters for signature and, as he signed them, she reminded him that there was a report he ought to look through.

'It will have to wait till tomorrow,' he said. 'I'm meeting my daughter-in-law at six and we're dining in Putney.'

'Oh, dear!' Miss Blockley said mildly.

'Yes.' Jason signed his usual slow, laborious signature.

'It must be lonely for Mrs York, poor little thing.'

'It is, very.' Jason took off his glasses and looked at Miss Blockley. 'I'm worried about her,' he said, 'but I think I can understand her unwillingness to leave that house. She had an unusual childhood, as you know, and I think her determination to stay there is a craving for security. The only security she has ever known has been there, with York. It's the only home she's had. It will take time to persuade her that the right thing is to sell up and to live somewhere else. I'm leaving things as they are for the time being, but I don't intend to let her stay there indefinitely.'

'It's such a horrible night.' Miss Blockley shuddered.

'I know.' Jason signed the last letter and got up. Miss Blockley helped him into his overcoat.

It was still dry as he walked round to the car park, but as he drove westwards along Piccadilly big blobs of sleet-like rain squashed themselves against the windscreen. It was just six o'clock as he slid past the top of Arlington Street. He scanned the Ritz arches, a few yards short of Green Park Station; Easter would almost certainly be sheltering. He stopped by the last arch and waited, looking back to see if she was coming. She was not.

Good, Jason thought. He was glad he had not kept her waiting. He watched the crowds pouring into the tube station; everyone looked preoccupied, frowning and red-nosed, in a hurry to get home.

A prostitute, wrapped like a parcel in mink, was doing her best to attract his attention from the pavement under the arches. Surely, Jason thought, he looked like a man waiting for a woman? He frowned at her and she answered with a good-natured wink.

Presently a policeman came up. He knew Jason well by sight. 'Good evening, sir.'

'I'm waiting for my daughter-in-law, Officer.'

'You haven't chosen a very good place, sir.'

'Good Lord!' Jason looked at the clock on the dashboard in astonishment. 'I'm supposed to meet her at six; it's six-fifteen now! She's not the sort of person who's ever late. Look, will you keep an eye on the car whilst I run back to my flat? She might possibly be there as the weather's so awful.'

Jason trotted down Arlington Street but, according to the commissionaire of the block of flats, no one had called, and there were no messages. Jason used the commissionaire's telephone to dial the Putney number, and waited. 'Ringing note, but no reply.'

He went off up Arlington Street hoping to find Easter already in the car. But she wasn't and now he was really worried and told the policeman so. It was the fear of the unknown, Jason thought, as he sat gloomily at the wheel. What were they up against? If it were never to be discovered who killed York, the rest of his life would be spent in being uneasy. Whenever he thought of York's death, he would have the crawling uneasy feeling in the gut that was real fear. He remembered a line from *Henry V* which he had learnt at school: 'Possess them not with fear; take from them now the sense of reckoning . . .'

And that was the heart of the matter, it was the result of his reasoning that was frightening him. So he must stop trying to think things out. A frightened fat man was no good to anyone, he thought.

And a frightened fat man, possessed by a thin one wildly signalling for help, is unseemly in theory. In fact, the prosperous businessman, wearing his Lock's bowler hat, sat in his elderly Rolls-Royce, frowning and biting the corner of a thumbnail.

A minute before half past six he started the engine, took a final look round, put the gear in and crept past the policeman, now standing at the entrance to the station, with an acknowledgement of his salute and went towards Putney as fast as he was able to drive.

He was driving over Putney Bridge just after a quarter to seven which, he thought, was surely a record in the rush hour. He had had York's keys in his pocket with his own ever since he had been through York's possessions and Easter knew he had them. If the house was in darkness he would let himself in; he did not quite know what he expected to find.

He turned off the busy main road, drove some few yards and then into the entrance to Silverdale. It was quite dark; though he could see cracks of light from behind closely drawn curtains in the other houses there was no light from Easter's house. He swept round the drive and stopped at the front door, his headlights illuminating the rhododendron bushes. He left the lights on and sat still for a moment. There was probably some perfectly simple reason for Easter's non-appearance. Her watch might have stopped, for instance. It was only a few minutes' walk from the cinema to the place they had arranged to meet, but she might have tried to get a taxi and failed, she might have fallen and sprained her ankle, she might have met an old friend. He should have waited a quarter of an hour longer.

But as he was here he might as well go inside and ... Jason shied away from the thought ... look round. He took York's bunch of keys out of his pocket. There were two mortice and two Yale keys, one of each for front and back doors. He did not know which was which so he left the door of the car open in order that the light should illuminate the entrance porch whilst he tried the keys. It didn't take a minute; the front door was opened and Jason put his hand inside and turned on the hall light. He was shaking. Just to show himself how normal he felt, he turned back to the car, switched out the lights, shut the heavy door carefully and went into the house, taking his ubiquitous despatch-case with him.

A wave of hot air met him. Perhaps the thermostat of the oil-fired boiler had gone wrong. It was certainly abnormally hot, but then, he remembered, Easter was inclined to over-heat the house; he had noticed it before. The sitting-room door was closed. Jason opened it and went in, switching on the lights. It looked charming; the curtains were drawn close and the small fireside table was laid for dinner for two with a lace tablecloth, fish knives and forks, the silver candlesticks from the dining-room, wine glasses and a Sheffield plate wine coaster. The fire had died down in the grate, but a filled coal box and log basket stood on either side of the fireplace. On the grog tray were clean glasses and a dish of olives.

Jason sighed with relief; the dear gal! Though she had left the house during the morning she had thought of everything, even to leaving the curtains cosily drawn. He would ring up the Ramsgates to see whether Jill had returned, and then, with his hand on the telephone receiver, he remembered that Jill was to stay in town for dinner and would not be coming home until late.

Smiling, he looked round. Everything was prepared for a delightful evening *à deux*. In a minute or two the telephone would ring and he would hear Easter's worried voice telling him what mishap had occurred. He would probably have to jump into the car and go to Putney Bridge Station and meet her.

In the meantime, Jason returned to the hall, took off his hat and peeled off his coat and scarf. Back in the sitting-room he stood in front of the bottles and wondered what he would have. He would mix a cocktail for them both. Knowing his liking for dry Martini, she had left a lemon and a small silver knife to cut the rind. Ice . . . in the fridge. He went across the hall and into the kitchen, switching on the light.

And then he stopped, his back tickling almost unbearably as though every small hair had come upright. He stood quite still, his hand on the switch, and listened. There was not a sound, not a creak. He shook himself irritably; this was the limit, he was becoming an hysterical old woman. He went across to the refrigerator, opened the heavy door and pulled out the ice tray, which he carried back into the sitting-room. He put several cubes of ice into the mixture and stirred it thoughtfully, round and round in the big glass beaker which York had used for mixing cocktails. Dear York, he thought, how fussy he was about detail. He had taken back to Fortnum and Mason the big cocktail shaker which a business friend had given him for a wedding present, and changed it for the glass beaker.

He poured a little of the cocktail into a glass and tasted it, added a little Vermouth, tasted it again, filled the glass, drank about half, went across to the fireplace, put the glass on the chimneypiece and knelt down in front of the fire. He put on a handful of small wood and taking the bellows he used them vigorously.

And when it happened he felt that he was having a *déjà vu*, the feeling that all this had happened before. He had always believed that time was a matter of relativity and this was now to be demonstrated in that it all seemed to happen so slowly. The first blow fell high, almost at the back of his neck, above the collar bone, and he thought: so that is where the first wound was! Unfortunately, that first blow was so violent that he crumpled forward, hitting his face on the logs he had put on the hot ashes and breaking two front teeth, which hurt a good deal more than the stab wound.

He was being stabbed again and again and he was not feeling any more pain but rushing down a long dark tunnel at the end of which was a bright light. He wanted very much to get to the light at the end of the tunnel but he knew that there was still something he must do.

He must turn round and see who was attacking him. But he was not able to. Only when he was nearly at the end of the tunnel was he able to look back over his shoulder and see, away back, a tiny, tiny thought, and it was: they are enjoying it, they like stabbing me, they like killing! But he did not feel surprise, or horror, or fear. He felt nothing but delight because he was so near the end of the tunnel now and nothing else mattered.

He left behind the fat man and the thin man and he was simply Jason as he went out into the light.

CHAPTER XVI

As Easter was stepping out of the train at East Putney Station, she caught the pencil heel of her shoes on the edge of the step. She succeeded in not falling and, looking round, she was dismayed to see the heel had become completely detached and was lying on the floor of the carriage from which she had alighted. A man picked it up and handed it to her politely and Easter, balancing on one leg, thanked him.

She proceeded towards the ticket collector at the station exit in a series of hops. She looked at the clock, which said twenty-five to eight. She waited until the crowd had passed through before handing him her ticket and saying: 'Look what's happened! Do you think someone could telephone for a taxi for me?'

'Phone box there,' he said gruffly, with a jerk of his head.

'Oh!' Easter opened her eyes very widely at him. 'Could you ring up for me, please? I haven't any coppers.'

'Bert,' the ticket collector shouted. 'Lady in trouble!'

Easter followed Bert to the office and stood on one leg whilst he telephoned for a cab. 'Thank you so much,' she said, and he was almost more grateful for the charming smile than for the half-crown she pressed into his hand. She sank heavily into a shabby small chair. 'Oh, dear, I'm so tired!' And she looked it. 'It's such a beastly day in town and I was going to meet someone who never turned up. I waited for ages!'

The exchange of pleasantries went on for a few minutes. Easter looked at the clock. 'Ten to eight, nearly!' she said. 'Do you think the taxi will have had time to get here?'

A porter accompanied her as she hobbled down the stairs and into the taxi.

When the taxi arrived at the house Easter cried: 'Oh, thank goodness!' as she saw the lights on and the Rolls in the drive. Carrying her broken shoe in one hand, she paid the man, thanked him and turned to the front door, calling: 'Co – oo – ee! I'm here!' She felt in her handbag for her keys. 'Jason,' she called as she fitted the Yale key into the lock. The taxi driver, unable to go right round the drive because of the Rolls, was having a little difficulty in reversing without running into the yard wall in the dark. He had several shots at it, revving up his engine noisily.

Easter went into the house. 'Jason,' she called again. 'What on earth happened to you?'

She threw her black suede gloves on to the hall table and went towards the sitting-room. The door was wide open; she could see everything from where she stood, on the threshold.

The taxi driver had succeeded in getting his crate round without damaging either it or the Rolls and was about to drive away when he heard the screams.

He cringed in his seat, feeling several sizes smaller, remembering with horror that this was the house where that murder had happened. Easter appeared at the door, silhouetted against the light, and scream after scream tore up the darkness. The taxi driver was shocked stone cold, as he afterwards said, by the terrifying sound of her screams. He'd had three years of jungle warfare against the Japs but nothing had ever scared him like those screams. The one thing that seemed important was not to see what she was screaming about so much as to stop the noise, and with this in view he climbed heavily from his driving seat.

But by now the neighbours were on the scene, husbands torn from the dining-table with food still in their mouths; there were half a dozen people.

'I've nothing to do with it,' the taxi driver kept protesting after he had had one fearful peep into the sitting-room.

'Nothing to do with me; I only brought the lady up from the station. That's all I did, just brought the lady up from the station.'

CHAPTER XVII

'If you ask me,' Police Constable Bacon said (he always prefaced his dissertations with 'if you ask me', possibly because nobody ever did,) 'this lot is a Special Branch job. International. That lot isn't murder, it's hashash – ashash – ashass – ' he cleared his throat and started again, calmly – 'assassination, that's what is is.'

'What's the difference between murder and ash ... what you said?' his wife asked dutifully.

'Murder's murder,' he said profoundly, 'but the other thing is done for a political cause, as it were. And it's not half as bad.'

'How can you say that!' his wife reproached him. 'When the son was murdered you wasn't half upset; you said you'd seen some sights in your time but nothing that got you like that job. Made you feel sick.'

'Maybe I'm getting more yewsed to it,' he suggested. 'But I reckon there's a lot behind this that'll never come out. Mind you, there's a lot more clues in this last murder.'

'A lot more? You reckoned there wasn't anything to go on last time.'

'Nor there was. No weapon, no fingerprints. This time there's a mackintosh left laying on the floor not far from the corpse.'

'Whoever would be so careless as to leave their mack?'

'It was left there on purpose. It was covered with blood. This Sir Jason Cragg was a bleeder, different to his son, York Cragg, who bled quietly to death. The blood spurted up out of his father. And the murderer didn't bother about cleaning himself up, he simply steps out of the mack and leaves it laying there on the floor.'

'What else?'

'He got in through the cloakroom window. They have what they call a downstairs cloakroom in these posh houses. A lavatory, no less, and this one's divided up, like. There's the lavatory and hand basin, excetera, divided from the rest, and the rest's a small room with hooks round the walls where they keep the golf clubs, and umbrellas and coats and macks and scarves, very ar-la. And that's got quite a big window, but higher up than most. This particular one's got opaque glass you can't see through, like you get in bathroom windows. It's a sash window and looks like it was always kept fastened. There's a radiator under the window what the murderer could step on when he climbed through, and down on to the floor, see? Well!' Police Constable Bacon sat back, his thumbs in his waistcoat armholes. 'Blow me if they ain't stuck two plasters like you get for backache on two panes outside the window. The window's made up of small panes of this size. They stuck two plasters, one under where the central catch is and the other to the left, next pane but one, where the burglar catch is, that's a kind of screw you screw in by hand. See?'

'No.'

'So's they could break the pane and get their hands in and undo the screw without making a sound! It's a regular burglar's trick, that is.'

'Then it was burglary?'

'No. That's the rum part of it. Unless the chap was out after some special document the police don't know nothing about, there's nothink he was out after. Nothink's been touched. No drawers opened, nothink.'

'Well, I never!' Mrs Bacon exclaimed. 'What else? You said there was a lot more clues.'

'I meant two. But if it had been snowing properly!'

'He wouldn't of done it.'

'That's true.' Sam Bacon was thoughtful. 'It does seem fate has got it against that young Mrs Cragg, I must say. They tell me she's all alone in the world. Makes your heart bleed to see her. Friends have taken her in for the present.'

'I wouldn't go back there if I was her.'

'It's her home, duck, when all's said and done. And there's people don't mind what's happened in a place just so's they've got somewhere to live. Ever heard of the housing shortage?'

But Police Constable Bacon was not feeling really flippant. 'Dear me,' he sighed, 'this was a dirty job, if ever there was one. There wasn't much of a fire, smouldering wood, but they left him with his face in the fire and when we pulled the poor devil round his face was black and burned and his front teeth broken and blood all over. But I don't know. Those two, father and son, they must of been up to somethink, I reckon. There's international gangs at the back of this. A foreign power.'

'Who, dear?' Mrs Bacon asked mildly.

Police Constable Bacon looked to right and to left in a distinctly cloak-and-dagger manner. 'Russia!' he hissed.

The Second Part

CHAPTER I

Nathaniel Sapperton lingered before the looking-glass on the dressing-chest in front of the window of the bedroom in the flat he had taken furnished on the edge of Putney Heath. He was not really worried about getting bald but it had become a habit to smooth his hand over the top of his head and quite often, as he did so, he was startled to find how little hair he had on top.

Forty-two, he told himself now, as he adjusted his bow-tie. Too old to be suspected of being Up To No Good, not old enough to be accused of being in his dotage; neither young wastrel nor elderly lecher; neither ne'er-do-well nor successful tycoon: what label could he wear? For a label was essential. Poet or writer? No, that would necessitate some evidence of achievement. Musician? He didn't know the first thing about music. Seafaring man? Captain in the Merchant Navy, perhaps? Soldier?

Leaning past the looking-glass, he peered once again through the net curtain down into the gardens of the recently-built houses called Silverdale below. The hose was still lying on the concrete of the yard but she had not yet returned from the house. She intended to come back, though, because she had left the water running; he could see it streaming down across the dry concrete to the central drain.

Drawing back into the room, he looked at himself in the glass; what did he look like? Dispassionately Mr Sapperton studied his face which he considered to be ordinary. But what could be more ordinary than one's own face? Something one has to see day in and day out, over the years, for a lifetime?

Mr Sapperton had two eyes, a nose and a mouth; 'po-faced' he had always considered himself to be. He was neither tall nor short, dark nor fair, his jaw was neither 'square' nor receding.

Dear me, he was so average that he had better stick to the truth, the plain, unglamorous truth. He was a civil servant attached to the Foreign Office and he was on leave after a special posting in the Persian Gulf.

There she was; she had evidently been into the house for a leather, for now she was vigorously wiping her car after the hosing.

He picked up his field-glasses from the dressing-chest and studied her through them. Her hair was tied round with a bright yellow scarf and she wore a mackintosh tightly gripped at the waist with a leather belt, and gumboots. She was energetically wiping her red MG over with wide vigorous strokes.

Lowering the field-glasses, Mr Sapperton reached across for the telephone which he now placed on the dressing-chest; he dialled a number, Putney 0909. OK so far; she left the leather on the bonnet of the car and hurried into the house. The ringing tone stopped as the receiver was lifted. 'Hallo?'

'Is that you, honey?' Mr Sapperton cooed softly.

'Who is that?' the voice answered sharply.

'It's me, Nat.'

'I'm afraid you've got the wrong number. This is Putney 0909.'

'Putney! Why, I dialled Riverside. I'm sorry.' Mr Sapperton managed to put not only a laugh into his reply but a slightly American accent; his own voice reminded him strongly of Gary Cooper's as he fluted: 'I'm saw-ry!'

'You've been mis-routed; you'd better replace your receiver and dial again.'

'I've been wha-at?'

'Mis-routed,' she repeated clearly.

'Have I, indeed? Mis-routed, well, well. Say, who are you, honey?'

'This is Mrs York Cragg speaking, I'm Putney 0909. Please replace your receiver.' There was a sharp click which came with the surprise of a small stab to Mr Sapperton, who thought he had been getting on so nicely.

She came out of her house and, picking up her leather, she renewed her wiping of the car even more energetically than before.

Mr Sapperton reconsidered the situation. It was important not to waste time and he might spend several days trying to get to know her. Her house was, for his particular requirements, so awkwardly placed; it was impossible to approach without a definite object in view. In fact, none of the ordinary methods of approach seemed feasible.

After a suitable pause he dialled again and watched her, once more, return to the house.

'Is that Mrs York Cragg? This is the bloke who's just been annoying you with – er – mis-routing. I say, I must apologize. Will you please forgive me? The fact is, you sounded so like someone I know, used to know, rather. Your voice, that is . . .' he began to babble, chattering on about a young woman he used to know at Riverside 0909 and how he was feeling kind of lonesome, coming back to this country after so long and not knowing anyone, and now he had discovered that this particular young woman had gone away and her flat was let to some people who couldn't even speak English. He did hope, he babbled feverishly, that Mrs Cragg would forgive his impertinence but just to hear a friendly voice meant a lot to him.

Not having the slightest idea as to what sort of person she was, made the essay a tremendous gamble. Some women would have slammed down the receiver in indignation, others, not. It would all depend on what sort of impression his voice made and to him his voice was as ordinary and unremarkable as was his face.

'Who are you?' she asked irritably when she was able to make herself heard.

'I'm Nathaniel Sapperton,' he cried eagerly. 'I've got a furnished apartment at Nero House, on Putney Heath; took it from a chap I know in the FO.'

'The what?'

'The FO. Foreign Office.' He burbled on.

He felt emanations of amusement from the end of the line and stopped abruptly. 'What's the joke, honey?'

'It's only that you're a neighbour.'

'Well, if that isn't a coincidence! What flat are you?'

'Not a flat. I live in one of those new houses you overlook, Silverdale, or perhaps you're on the other side of the block, facing the Heath, are you?'

'Why, I must be looking down on you right now! The sitting-room faces the Heath, but the bedroom . . . I'm on the third floor, next to the top. You don't say!'

They both laughed.

'Well,' she paused, 'goodbye, for now.' She put down the receiver, but gently this time.

But this time it was all right. Mr Sapperton grinned cheerfully at himself in the looking-glass; not that there was really very much to smile about, but it is always delightful when deep-laid schemes come off.

There was a photograph of a woman on his dressing-chest; he gave her a copious wink before putting it away in a drawer under his clean shirts.

Clearly she was half expecting him; the car was now quite dried off, but she was polishing vigorously at the chromium with a dry duster. Nothing was said that was not entirely conventional but, behind the commonplace exchange of words, each was eyeing the other with the alertness of the unattached male and female meeting for the first time.

He thought: yes, she's pretty, but there is something more interesting there. Her manner was warm and friendly enough, he considered her distinctly charming, but there was a detachment about her comparable to that of a pretty hospital nurse. There was that something else about her, which, for the moment, he found indefinable.

He picked up a duster and for some minutes he helped her to polish. He stood back, finally, and remarked that it was a very pretty little car and split new, he felt sure. Yes, she told him, she had had it only a few weeks. It had been a present from her father-in-law who, as a matter of fact, had never seen it. It arrived after he had died.

Mr Sapperton clicked his tongue. Wasn't it a pity, now, he observed.

Easter tossed the duster down and pulled off her cleaning gloves. 'Thank you for helping me, Mr Sapperton. Now, the least I can do is to ask you in for a drink. Do come; it's nearly six o'clock.'

Protesting that it was not his habit to accept drinks from ladies, Mr Sapperton followed her eagerly enough into the house. In silence she mixed a cocktail in the glass mixer and it was only when she raised her glass to him and met his puzzled look that she said: 'Doesn't the name Cragg convey anything to you?'

Mr Sapperton settled himself comfortably into an armchair. 'Out there in the Persian Gulf, where I've come from, you get a bit out of touch,' he explained chattily. 'What with the heat, and all the drink one consumes; it's not that you feel so far from home as that you get things, and by things I mean the film and book reviews, the news of what's going on in Parliament, and so on, all a bit out of focus. They don't seem to matter much out there in the heat and you're too darned hot to understand them, anyway.'

'But the ordinary news.'

Mr Sapperton's face appeared to undergo a series of convolutions before it more or less righted itself. 'Isn't that, Cragg . . . do you mean the Golden Fleece Cragg . . . I mean to say . . . that is . . .'

He had the weirdest feeling about her; it seemed almost as though she were being deliberately modest, like a famous actress who has just allowed her real identity to slip out. He was shaken with a shudder, as though the small hairs on his spine were suddenly sprouting.

He watched her smile that was not a smile but a curious downwards turning of one side of the mouth, accompanied by a lowering of the eyelids. It was the look of slightly sneering modesty exactly similar to that which Mr Sapperton had, from time to time, observed upon the face of the Mona Lisa: 'Here I am, a famous character, through no fault of my own; look as much as you like, you clots, you won't be any the wiser.' He had never been an admirer of Leonardo's heroine.

'Well —' she shrugged slightly — 'you would have wondered where my husband was. Better to tell you straight away.'

'Quite.' He gulped down the rest of his drink. 'Quite.' And stood up to go.

Easter filled his glass. 'Don't take fright,' she said. 'I'm enjoying having you here. I'm probably more lonely than you are. I've a daily woman who comes in the mornings, and my friends the Ramsgates live not far away, but still I am lonely. Horrible things happening to people seems to make them lonely. It singles them out, and if other people are sorry for them and are kind to them it still gives them the feeling of being isolated. One is the Kind of Person that Things Happen to. "That poor Easter Cragg." Do I sound sorry for myself? I am, rather.'

'Let me get this straight. Somebody killed both your husband and his father? Stabbing, was it?'

She nodded. 'And the verdict was murder by person or persons unknown, which means the police can go on "investigating", that is, interviewing thousands of people, or rather, getting them to fill in forms stating where they were and when, and looking into the movements of every known criminal in the country . . . and out of it. "Nation-wide probe" they may call it. Every now and then the papers publish a small paragraph telling how busy the police are and at any moment now there's going to be an arrest. It'll go on just until there have been enough new murders to take people's minds off the stale ones, and then it'll be dropped. UNSOLVED, I suppose they'll write in their files.'

Mr Sapperton drank his second cocktail in one gulp, murmuring something a little unintelligible about not being surprised she felt embittered, it was a dreadful thing, really dreadful . . .

'Don't get me wrong,' she said with a sharp little laugh, 'I only want them to drop it *now*. Why can't they let sleeping dogs lie?'

'Don't you want them to discover the criminal?'

'Not at the expense of laying bare Jason and York's private lives for everyone to see, chew over, speculate upon.'

He nodded sympathetically. 'I think I understand.'

'I don't believe in the eye-for-an-eye principle, it's out of date. Besides, people don't get murdered for nothing.'

'How do you mean?'

'Well, I mean . . . somebody evidently thought both Jason and York needed to be murdered. And if they have done something that is so wrong and wicked . . . well, they're dead, let's not tell the whole world about it!'

For a long time Mr Sapperton was quiet, leaning against the chimneypiece with his empty glass in his hand, idly kicking a log in the hearth with the toe of his shoe.

'Of course, you may take an exactly opposite view, like my friends John and Jill Ramsgate. They think the criminal should be discovered at all costs; they want me to offer a huge reward for information that may lead to the discovery of the murderer. What do you think?'

'I . . .' Mr Sapperton was obliged to clear his throat.

'I'm not sure what I think. I'd like to know a lot more about it.'

'So would I.'

'I mean, I'd like to know at least as much as everyone else,' Mr Sapperton corrected himself. 'I did read about it, of course, but now that I've met you the whole thing looks different.'

'It's taken on a more personal aspect, I expect. All at once you see that I'm a real person and not simply one of those newspaper characters whose relations, husbands, lovers, gets murdered. I suppose that's what you mean.'

'In a way. Do you mind if I look up the recent newspaper reports?'

'Are you one of those people who are passionately interested in murder, then, Mr Sapperton?'

'By no means, but you asked my opinion just now.'

There was the very slightest suggestion of a pout about her full, babyish mouth as she looked down into her empty glass. What lovely eyelids she has, Mr Sapperton thought, so young!

'Are you here all alone?' he asked.

'I suppose you're thinking: "How could she!" A lot of people do. The Ramsgates can't understand it. But it's my home. The only home I've ever had.'

He looked down at the hearth.

She nodded. 'Yes, Jason was killed right there, where you're standing.' She added after a moment: 'I haven't much imagination,' as though in some surprise.

There seemed to be nothing adequate Mr Sapperton could find to say.

'I'm sorry,' she said at last and put out a small hand to touch his own. It was cold, like the touch of a dead mouse's claw. 'When you left your flat and came out to find me, you probably felt gay and cheerful. We might have had lots of fun together . . . that is . . . if things had been different.'

Now was the time to say: 'You poor kid, etc., etc.' But somehow or other Mr Sapperton could not. He was too shocked or . . . something. He could not say it. He looked at her with an oddly helpless, where-do-we-go-from-here look.

'Don't think I mind talking about it,' Easter went on. 'Go away and look it all up at *The Times* office in the last few weeks' papers. Then we can talk it over, talk it out of the way, perhaps.'

'And have fun after all,' he suggested sadly.

CHAPTER II

In the movie there were two American businessmen shooting off their mouths at each other, and there was a gorgeous blonde, top-heavy with outsize breasts, teetering between them, firing off wisecracks with a babyish lisp but, though he did not take his eyes from the screen, Mr Sapperton did not see or hear anything at all, he was entirely absorbed in his thoughts.

Going over the simple facts of the two murders there seemed to be not one single definite conclusion arising from them. Though it was probable, it was not safe to say that both the murders were done by one man, or that they were both done by one man unaided by someone else.

Was it a plot or a plan? A plot pre-supposes more than one person engaged, a plan would be the intended proceedings of one person. If the first murder had been either plotted or planned, it showed little signs of either. It could have been unpremeditated. In the second murder, there were distinct signs of plot or plan. There was the burglar's trick of the plaster on the cloakroom window which could have been arranged either before or *immediately after*. There was also the grey plastic mackintosh which did not necessarily prove either plot or plan. Snow clouds had been gathering the whole of that day, and early in the morning after the murder, snow had fallen heavily; anyone might have been wearing a plastic mackintosh over a warm coat.

On both occasions it appeared that the murdered man was alone in the house; Mr Sapperton had a curiously strong impression arising from this fact; he could see a watcher outside the house, hands deep in the pockets of his coat, possibly already holding the knife, hat pulled down over the face. The house, almost buried up to the eaves in its banks of mournful evergreen, could be watched so easily by someone entirely concealed.

Someone who knew a good deal about the Cragg movements. Someone, for instance, who knew that York was alone in the house when his wife and friends had left for London. Someone who knew that Jason Cragg was alone when he let himself into the house before Easter's return, with his dead son's key. Someone who found it a great deal more convenient to stab Jason Cragg in his daughter-in-law's house in Putney than in his own flat in Arlington Street, within eyeshot of the commissionaire. Understandable, that.

The first murder was done, undoubtedly, by someone whom York knew, or someone who had a password which caused York to let him into the house.

At the inquest on York Cragg, his friend, John Ramsgate, giving evidence, had said that he thought York was suffering from a perfectly ordinary cold and headache such as we all had from time to time. He had told him that he didn't feel well but that he did not want to spoil their evening; as they were starting out he had evidently not felt up to a dinner in the West End. His father had also said that, when he had had the telephone conversation with York, he had told him that he was not feeling too well, a cold, or something, but that he hoped to be all right for the business trip. The evidence thus showed that York's evening alone at home was not prearranged.

The second murder – for the moment Mr Sapperton discounted the larks at the cloakroom window – could have been done in exactly the same way. The watcher could have waited until Sir Jason had opened the front door, returned to his car to put out the lights, gone into the house and shut the front door, before approaching. He could then have rung the front door bell; Sir Jason, having taken off his hat and coat, would open it and the visitor would say something which would cause Sir Jason to invite him inside on this cold night. Inside, and into the living-room, where Sir Jason would mix a drink for them both, pouring some into his own glass and tasting it before stooping to attend to the fire. It was then that the visitor would strike, high up, as before. And when it was all over he would step out of his blood-drenched mackintosh and leave it lying on the floor. The plasters on the outside of the cloakroom window and the unfastening of the catches could be completed in three minutes; the murderer could slip away, out into the darkness and the wilds of South London and be lost for ever.

The police enquiries into the plastic mackintosh could not lead anywhere; the manufacturers reported weekly sales of some ten thousand, all exactly similar; they were sold in their hundreds at the price of a guinea each at all big stores and a great many small ones all over the country.

Since the Craggs' public life allowed of as much concealment as the inside of a bird cage, the guiding principle of both the murders must lie in their private life, and about that, Mr Sapperton was sure, Mrs Easter Cragg must know something. Something.

The view she was taking about 'letting sleeping dogs lie' was absurd and, moreover, primitive. Was there the suggestion of the wronged woman about the beautiful Easter? Like all women, Mr Sapperton thought irritably, she confused the issue. Didn't she realize that it was far more dreadful to have your husband and your father-in-law revengefully stabbed to death than to have their private lives ripped wide open and exposed to public gaze? That the one must follow the other was a self-evident inference; if it turned out that there was nothing discreditable in their private lives, well and good, if not – not. It was an equal chance. And if it proved to be the case and there was something which would involve Easter in a loss of repute, she would have to put up with it. Murder was desperate and final, and finding the answer to it allowed for no consideration of the feelings of a sensitive and lady-like young woman.

And thus, having reached at least one definite conclusion by a process of careful reasoning, Mr Sapperton was aware that he was looking into the eyes of the blonde in a head some three hundred or so times bigger than his own and in a tremendously loud, husky whisper she was saying: 'You need me, darling, as much as I need you.'

CHAPTER III

'And so you see,' Mr Sapperton said, 'so long as these murders remain unexplained, you'll never really have a happy moment.'

'Oh, I don't know.' Easter, with lowered lids, pressed out the butt of her cigarette. 'I'm happy now, for instance. I'm even having what you might call a lovely time.' She looked round the little Chinese restaurant at which they were dining, and sipped her hot milk-less tea.

Mr Sapperton shook his head. 'It's nice of you to put it like that, but I know you're not really happy, you can't be. You're a nice girl, and a brave girl, if I may say so, and you don't believe in making a fuss. But you're never going to be really happy, inside, till you know who did the murders, and why.'

'All right, if you say so.' Easter smiled amiably. 'But

perhaps foundlings look at things differently.'

'All this crap about foundlings, and by the way, it's a dreadfully out-of-date appellation. You've got a Victorian streak in you that positively revels in being what you insist on calling a "foundling".'

He flipped open his lighter as Easter helped herself to another cigarette. 'You don't mind my saying these things, do you?'

'Not at all. Everybody likes talking about their fascinating selves.'

'Well, as I say, all this crap about foundlings. Move with the time, girl. Every other home, these days, is a broken one.'

Easter pursed her lips in a disbelieving hiss.

'Well, almost. The family as a unit doesn't amount to anything now. All the high-falutin' talk about security and happy-faces-round-the-fire – ' Mr Sapperton flicked his fingers in dismissal – 'a lot of hoo-ey. Children are brought up to consider no one but themselves and I dare say it will turn out to be as good a generation as we've ever had.'

'That's a matter of opinion, and you're slightly drunk,' Easter observed.

'I don't think you've suffered in the least from being an orphan,' Mr Sapperton, undeflated, declared.

'I may not have suffered, exactly,' Easter said slowly, 'but I'm different.'

'Everyone likes to think they're different. In what way are you different?'

'I'm an entity on my own, with no background. It does make a difference, you know. I live for the present. And that is why it is really true when I say I'm happy *now*. I haven't gradually emerged from my childhood as an integrated person. No one has ever been anything but kind and sweet to me but in an impersonal way, so that my character hasn't been formed out of *anything*; am I putting it clearly? I haven't evolved, opened out, developed, like a normal child. I'm merely a skin containing all the characteristics I was born with in adult form.'

'So what?' Mr Sapperton asked crudely.

'So – I'm different.'

Mr Sapperton took her small hand, which lay unemployed upon the tablecloth. 'You're not all that different, as they say, but go on thinking so, if you want. And I'll go on thinking you're not happy. We don't have to think the same way about everything to get on fine, do we?' He forced her to smile back at him.

'If I'm not happy, I'm feeling extremely comfortable inside after all that exciting food. And this delicious jasmine tea – I could drink gallons of it.' She helped herself to more.

'Now listen – ' Mr Sapperton took some more tea himself – 'you foundling. I think you need some help; you're so awfully alone. And being a natural busy-body with a few weeks of idleness ahead of me, I think I'm the bloke to help you. Do you want me to?'

'Of course.'

'Well, then, will you take my advice?'

'That depends.'

'On what?'

'On whether I think it's good or not.'

'Well, I'm damned! I want you to telephone to the press, the *Daily Gape* if you like, and tell them you're offering a reward for information leading to the arrest of the person, or persons, who murdered your husband and his father. And make it a good big one.'

'Oughtn't it to be done through a solicitor?'

'If you like. Certainly, if you want. But it is important that the so-called cheap press should make a big thing of it.'

'But the past few weeks have been one long struggle to avoid the reporter from the *Daily Gape* and some of the Sunday papers too. They've even offered me money to write an article about my life with York Cragg.'

'All the better. All you have to do is to make the simple statement; you are offering a reward of so-and-so. It doesn't mean you have to throw open your doors to their sexi-rama boys.'

'I'll have to think about it.'

Mr Sapperton stirred uneasily. 'Nothing ages as rapidly as a murder case. There is at least one person in this world who at this moment is congratulating himself that it's "all died down". The police are busy on new murders now, and we've a limited police force, after all. There's got to come a time when investigation slackens, and that's the time for the reward. Five thousand pounds for information that leads directly to an arrest. Somebody, other than the murderer, must know something.'

'What makes you say that?'

'Well, it's obvious.'

Easter looked puzzled. 'I don't see it at all.'

'Look, there must be someone who knows something, or who has their suspicions.'

'Give me an example of the sort of thing you mean.'

'Use your imagination.'

'I haven't any, I told you.'

'Well, someone's *behaviour*, for instance. You don't walk in from stabbing a man, hang up your hat, eat a good supper and settle down to watching the TV without showing some kind of stress.'

'Don't you?'

'Then there's the odd bloodstain. Don't tell me that first murder took place without there being any blood anywhere on the assailant's clothes. And there's the knife. Someone must have bought or stolen a knife. Or even used the family carving knife which must have been missing for a while anyway. Oh, I sound too damn silly; I had no idea I had it in me. I ought to write thrillers!'

'You're absolutely sure, aren't you, that someone other

than the murderer must know something?'

'Yes, I am.'

'Well, I don't agree.'

'Then that will have to be another point on which we disagree. You may be right, and if you are right, then your Five Thousand Pounds will remain intact, unclaimed,' he ended triumphantly.

A full minute passed.

'All right,' Easter agreed at last. 'I'll do what you say. I must telephone to the family solicitor first and make sure that it's all right. The estate isn't anything like settled yet, and I dare say if that Five Thousand Pounds were to be awarded to an informant, he would get it put down on some expense account, and not let it be liable for Income Tax or Death Duties, or something.' Easter smiled. 'How's that?'

'Fine.'

For once Easter had driven to London in her MG which she had parked nearby. They left the Chinese restaurant and walked arm in arm to the garage in Brewer Street.

'Sure you wouldn't like to go to a movie or anything?'

'Isn't it getting a bit late?'

'Late for a movie, perhaps, but too soon to go home.'

'I'd like to see your flat.'

'You would!' Mr Sapperton looked down at her, delighted by the implication. She looked lovely and smelled lovely, was she going to *be* lovely?

CHAPTER IV

No, not quite that, but Mr Sapperton was convinced that it was all due to carelessness on his part that their dinner at the Chinese restaurant did not culminate in a night of love. Sheer carelessness, for before leaving he forgot to put away his newly acquired vintage Rolls-Royce in the communal garage beneath the block of flats and when Easter swung round the gravel drive in front of Nero Court in her MG with Mr Sapperton beside her, the old black-and-cream Rolls lay there, in the drive, as portly and dignified as ever.

She stopped in front of the lighted portico and Mr Sapperton could see her face. She was staring at the Rolls as though at something obscene and her face was the colour of a mid-day December sky.

'What's wrong?' he asked sharply.

'My father-in-law's car,' she choked.

'No, mine.'

'They told me it had been sold through the solicitors!'

'And I bought it. It's only a coincidence, honey; no need to upset yourself.'

'But it's a fantastic coincidence,' Easter declared.

'All coincidences are fantastic. When I got home from the Middle East I stayed at the little hotel off St James's Street I always use; I happened to go with a friend to collect his car from that big underground garage in Arlington Street and saw this job. Said I'd like to buy it if there was a chance and a few days later a car salesman rang me up and I had a trial run in it and it was fixed. Nobody told me the owner had been murdered. Thought it might put me off, I dare say.'

'My father-in-law's name will be in the logbook,' Easter exclaimed, a trifle wildly.

Mr Sapperton took her hand, which was icy cold. ' "Your tiny hand is frozen," ' he murmured whimsically. 'I dare say it will, but I don't read logbooks; I haven't even looked in it. But I have blown the bulb horn, boom! Sounds like the *Queen Liz* coming up Southampton Water, or a cow in labour.'

'It's the most extraordinary coincidence I ever heard: I can't get over it.'

'I could tell you of two or three even more extraordinary. It's a tiny world.'

But Easter did not seem to want to hear them. She sat limply at the driving wheel as though all the strength had gone out of her. Mr Sapperton leaned over and turned off the engine.

'Like to have a better look at her? I'm proud of her, you know.'

'No, thanks. I know every inch of it. He let me drive it often.'

'Then let's go in,' Mr Sapperton said brightly.

But the evening was shattered, there was no more fun to be had. She didn't want to see his flat now; all she wanted was to go home, to bring the evening to a close. He stayed with her until her car was put away and she had opened her own front door. It was obvious, after she had switched on the hall light, that she was trembling.

'You don't want me to come in, do you?'

She shook her head. 'No, I'm tired.'

He looked anxiously past her into the house. 'Do you really not mind being here alone?'

'Not a bit,' she murmured, 'but I suppose everything has left me nervy. It is sudden shock I don't like, I've had so many lately. I never used to be like this. People with no imagination don't usually suffer from nerves.'

'But look what you've been through.' Mr Sapperton wished very much they might go inside and continue this conversation in the warmth of the living-room. But Easter had no such intention; she was withdrawing gradually so that now she was inside and he was not and she was gently but slowly and firmly shutting the door.

'And you won't forget,' he reminded her urgently, 'what you're going to do in the morning. The *Daily Gape*, remember . . .'

'Good night, and thank you for the evening,' she said politely, and shut the door.

CHAPTER V

Police Constable Bacon had had a busy day. It was not until late in the evening that he got home from work and was able to relax in front of the telly. He picked up the *Daily Gape*.

'Cor, strike me dead!' he begged.

'There you are, Sam Bacon, there's your chance,' his wife laughed.

But PC Bacon did not see the joke. 'Five Thousand Pounds!' he muttered, more than once. 'What couldn't we do with Five Thousand, eh, Doris, girl?'

'We could use it,' Mrs Bacon said temperately.

'And how, we could use it! A smallholding on Purley Downs, eh? A second-hand Austin pick-up to take the veg to market, eh? We'd be all right, you and me. No need to worry about our old age and not having no kids to keep us. Yes, we'd be all right.' Police Constable Bacon was thoughtful.

'Have you got any ideas, then, Sam? I mean, could you supply any information leading to the arrest of the chap who done it?'

'Could I?' The Sam Bacon of a generation or so ago would have spat into the fire. Our Sam Bacon simply scratched himself. 'Could I?' he asked the cat.

'Perhaps it don't apply to a member of the Force.'

'Look, girl. How could I have any information on the QT? This is to tempt somebody who knows something. An accessory, maybe, another crook who'll turn Queen's Evidence.'

'Five Thousand Pounds,' Mrs Bacon mused, 'it's as good as winning a football pool. You was right on the spot, Sam.

Up to the neck in it, you were.'

'Too right,' he snarled, 'but I didn't see the bloomin' murders. I was just a few minutes too late!'

Mrs Bacon enjoyed prodding Sam into angry sarcasm born of the ingrained feeling of dissatisfaction with himself. It was her own peculiar way of reviving his far too latent ambitions.

'When your brain gets working, Sam, you never know. Do you, Puss?' she asked in her turn the cat. 'You never know what might happen!'

'All right,' Sam said bitingly, 'I'll put on me thinking cap, you never know . . .'

CHAPTER VI

Mr Sapperton did nothing until the evening of the day that the news of the reward was published. Then he telephoned.

'Well done! Now we shall see what we shall see.'

'Nothing's happened so far,' Easter returned.

'Don't expect somebody is going to rush round to the newspaper office the minute he's read about the reward. He'll take time to think it over. The police will be smothered under a whole heap of false clues. There'll be some wonderful feats of imagination.'

'The chief inspector called on me again today. I think, on the whole, they're pleased. He didn't tell me anything, of course.'

'He'd nothing to tell.'

'He was very mysterious about their various "lines of enquiry".'

'He would be. What are you doing, Easter?'

'Nothing.'

'Nothing?'

'Well, reading, actually.'

'Reading! I couldn't be more surprised. May I come round?'

'Yes, do. I'll make some coffee.'

She was wearing a long red woollen dressing-gown affair, when he arrived. The living-room curtains were closely drawn and the fire was blazing cheerfully.

'This is all very nice and cosy,' he said appreciatively. 'What are you reading?' He picked up a glossy magazine. There was a large pile of them on a small table.

Tonight Easter was all woman; she looked soft and warm and friendly. But only friendly.

'What have you been doing today?'

'Jill and I went to a dress show. Hartnell's spring collection.'

'Jill?'

'Jill Ramsgate.'

'Tell me about your friends the Ramsgates.'

'I don't know what I should do without them,' Easter said warmly. 'They took me to stay with them after . . . after Jason. It was Jill whom I was with at the movies the day I had arranged to meet him.'

The evening was going nicely. Mr Sapperton had his own idea about how it would have ended had it not been, this time, for the fateful telephone call.

This particular evening, for the first time, he felt something for Easter that more nearly approached real concern and affection. He had thought her easy of approach but difficult to get to know, an odd anomaly. But this evening he told himself he had been unfair. How could one sum up fairly any young woman who had just emerged from the experiences that had befallen Easter?

With the coffee tray balanced on the pile of magazines on the low table in front of them, they sat side by side on the big sofa, close together, and Mr Sapperton had a very real stab of remorse. Playing with her fragile-looking hand, he said sadly: 'I'm old enough to be your father.'

'Only just, surely. I like men a lot older than myself. York was nine years older than I. And Jason . . .'

'Did you like Jason?'

'Yes.'

'How much?'

'I could have married him.'

'Did he ask you to?'

'He didn't have time.'

Mr Sapperton was shocked into a full minute's silence. 'I couldn't be more surprised,' he said lightly.

'Jason *had* something. He was a fascinating man. So successful and yet so . . . so . . .'

'Humble?'

'That's it. Humble. How did you guess? Boyishly enthusiastic too, and almost uncertain of himself at times. So different from York. In fact, York seemed years older than his father. Jason had that youthful freshness you can't kill. I mean . . .' she paused. 'I mean, he didn't seem old. It was all such a pity, such a damn pity.' She changed her position, tucking her feet up into her long skirt. 'Now you tell me something,' she begged comfortably.

'Are you going to turn out to be one of those tiresome women who ask personal questions?' But the affectionate look he gave her took away any sting from his words. 'All right, I'll talk. But people who ask personal questions don't expect to get the whole truth,' he laughed gently.

> 'I remember, I remember,
> The house where I was born
> The little window where the sun
> Came peeping in at morn . . .' he began.

And then: 'No, you only want to know if I'm married, don't you? That's the only thing a woman every really wants to know about a man she meets, isn't it?'

Easter nodded.

The telephone stood on a little round Georgian wine table between the fireplace and the sofa, within an arm's length. There was an alabaster lamp, softly shaded in pale peach with an ivory-silk fringe on the same table, and a Sunderland saucer that was used as an ashtray. The telephone sat, squat and brooding, the Villain of the Piece and about to break up the evening so that nothing was ever the same again.

Mr Sapperton felt wildly silly, he might have been playing for time: *'I was born one wet Whit Monday, in a studio near the Boltons,'* he quoted.

' "Airs on a Shoe-string", darling,' Easter reproached him. 'It isn't as though you'd had anything to drink, not here, anyway.'

'As a matter of fact,' Mr Sapperton began, and when people start a sentence with 'as a matter of fact' it is always suspect, 'I married at twenty-four and was divorced at thirty. She divorced me, so now you see what you're up against.'

Being quite literally up against him, Easter laid her head on his shoulder and at this crucial moment the telephone rang. 'It'll be Jill, about tomorrow. We're going to another dress show if she can get Nannie to change her day.' She picked up the receiver: 'Putney 0909. Yes, this is Mrs York Cragg. Who are you? *Who?*'

Quack, quack, quack! Mr Sapperton heard. Quack, quack!

Easter put her hand over the mouth-piece. 'Oh, God!' 'Who is it?'

Easter shook her head, staring at him. 'I don't know. A man, a common voice. He wants to come.'

'Lord!' Mr Sapperton leaped up, gesticulating wildly. 'Tell him to come. Give us ten minutes to get the police,' he whispered.

Easter spoke back into the mouth-piece. 'Are you there?

One minute, please.' Her voice was husky with fear. Once more all the colour and vitality had drained out of her face with the rapidity of water running out of a hand-basin. 'It's he! It's the murderer. That must be how he phoned first York and then Jason, *and now me!*' she whispered. 'He says he's in the phone box at Putney Bridge Station.'

Mr Sapperton pressed his fist against his front teeth in an effort to think clearly. 'Tell him to come along.'

'You can get the bus from near the station to the corner of the road,' Easter said into the mouth-piece, evidently in reply to a question. 'But please give us a quarter of an hour. We . . .'

'We're just finishing our meal,' Mr Sapperton hissed.

Easter repeated his words into the mouth-piece and replaced it.

'What are we going to do?'

'You're going up to change out of that dressing-gown affair and I'm going to fix us both a stiff whisky. Hurry!'

But Mr Sapperton was in a state of indecision. Whisky in one hand, he paused with the other hand on the receiver. Should he or should he not ring up the police? They would arrive in their car, blocking up the drive and scaring the visitor away. Was it, in fact, the murderer, returning inevitably, or was it . . . of course, it was, someone who wanted to claim the Five Thousand reward!

He said as much when she came down. He smiled, calm now, and reassuring. 'This will be the first of many. Here, drink this. Why didn't we think of it? You'll be snowed under with mysterious phone calls, letters, callers. All they've got to do is to look you up in the telephone directory. You'll have all the crackpots and cranks in England after you, proposing marriage and heaven knows what else.'

'That reward was a shocking mistake.'

'Wait and see. Let's wait and see.'

'Oh, Nat! Hadn't you better get the police?'

'I've been thinking, better not. You said *us*, Easter, you wise child. Did you do it purposely? He knows you're not alone.'

Easter had drunk her whisky and soda; she was feeling much better. 'But isn't it wonderful that you happen to be here?' she said. 'I'd have been scared out of my wits if I'd been alone.'

'Perhaps that'll teach you,' he murmured.

'What?'

'Not to be alone.'

Easter wandered nervously about the room. 'He said his name was Ernest Millage. He had a thin cockney voice. He was nervous, he called me Miss.'

Easter stopped in front of him and looked at him with that particularly wide-eyed candid look which he knew was something to be careful of, in a woman. 'Have you ever heard of Ernest Millage?'

'No,' he said, looking equally directly at her. 'Give me a sheet of writing paper, Easter. I'm going to do something very amateurish and schoolboyish. A Precaution. I'm certain this is only a visitor about the reward, but this house has had one too many mysterious visitors coming here out of the night.'

With his fountain-pen Mr Sapperton wrote:

8.50 p.m. A mysterious cockney voice has just telephoned to Mrs York Cragg, asking to see her. He states that he is at Putney Bridge Station and is now on his way to the house. I am with her and we are awaiting his arrival.

He made a hieroglyphic at the bottom of the paper.

'Why don't you sign it?'

'This is in case he takes out a gun and shoots us both; they'll know who is meant by *I*.'

Mr Sapperton went out of the room and Easter helped

herself to another whisky from the grog tray.

'Where have you put it?' she asked on his return.

'I've slipped it inside the kitchen table drawer, where you keep all your cooking knives and things. He'll be unlikely to look there, if he ever gets round to ransacking the house. But the police look everywhere. It's all right, dearest girl, nothing is going to happen. It's simply a silly little man called Ernest Millage with a bit of useless information. Here he is . . .'

Mr Sapperton had shattered the intimate atmosphere of the sitting-room by switching on the brilliant ceiling-light before opening the front door. Ernest Millage stood pale and blinking, a little dirty and ill-looking in the ruthless light. He was clearly very nervous, jerking forward like a puppet and holding out his hand to Easter. 'Mrs Cragg? Pleased to meet you.'

'This is Mr Sapperton, a friend of the family,' Easter indicated.

'Pleased to meet you.' Mr Millage shook hands spasmodically.

Easter looked completely mystified. 'I'm afraid I've no idea who you are, Mr Millage.' She did not look frightened now, nor particularly worried; Ernest Millage did not have the appearance of any sort of monster. He was short and good-looking in a white-mouse-faced way. He had a large nose and a slightly receding chin and his eyes were faintly pink-rimmed. He was wearing an exaggeratedly smart and inexpensive overcoat and a coloured silk muffler and would clearly have looked more comfortable in a grubby raincoat.

When he said that his attention had been caught by the announcement of the reward that was being offered for information leading to the arrest of the murderer of the Craggs, father and son, the tension was relaxed. Mr Sapperton asked him to sit down and Easter offered him the open cigarette-box. There was an exchange of pleasantries about how far Mr Millage had come, the frequency of the buses and the cold wind that had sprung up. And then an awkward pause.

Looking tensely at the glowing end of his cigarette, Ernest Millage said that it was about his wife. He had only been married a couple of years and he realized that his wife had never done what you might call settle down, if they understood his meaning. But he'd read all about these enticement cases, as they called them, and he understood full well that he was the victim of some such case. His wife had never been *allowed* to settle down, and now she'd been enticed away altogether and Mr Millage was not going to rest until he'd found her. The poor girl wasn't herself, it was like she was hypnotized. 'She always did have ideas above her station,' Mr Millage said gloomily.

It was such a surprising outlook that Easter and Nat exchanged amused glances.

'You must have a drink, Mr Millage,' Nat said, going across to the grog tray.

'No, thanks, I'm a teetotaller,' he returned aggressively, and lapsed into a savage brooding. Easter raised her eyebrows to Nat, and shrugged her shoulders slightly, and Nat, who had taken the opportunity of giving himself another drink, stood glass in hand before the fire, waiting, with a receptive look on his face, for Mr Millage to continue. Which, presently, he did.

His Valentine, he said, was an actress and his mother had warned him, many a time and oft, of the danger of marrying an actress. But she was so sweet, so sweet . . .

Easter and Nat both looked away from the pitiful sight of Mr Millage struggling with tears. He pulled himself together and went on. He knew full well, when he married her, that she'd a past, but then, so had he, neither of them were exactly chickens. But they had each agreed to ignore the other's past. Valentine was ready, even eager, to settle down and have a kiddie or two. They'd found a nice little house in Edgware and he'd gone off to work every day, leaving her as happy, as he thought, as a cricket, with her chores. But oh dear me no! She'd been up to all sorts of larks behind his back. Lunches in the West End . . . all sorts.

Easter and Nat again exchanged amused glances as words failed Mr Millage as to the precise form of the larks.

There were no kiddies, that was the trouble, no kiddies. If there'd been a baby she'd have given Mr York Cragg and all the rest of them the bird.

'Just a minute, not so fast,' Mr Sapperton exclaimed. 'You can't make statements like that. Mr York Cragg spent this last year in getting engaged and marrying.'

Ernest Millage put his hand inside his coat and brought out a large envelope.

'This is a copy which his father Sir Jason Cragg had made of a photograph he found amongst his son's possessions, of my wife. He had three made in all, so there's two others somewhere. A photograph taken, mind you, without my knowledge only a bit above a year ago. Last February, to be precise. There was some writing on the photograph, great big actressy writing (as though she was *somebody*) and that has come out on the copy, large as life. Like to see it?' Millage's voice trembled under the weight of his bitterness and his hands shook perceptibly as he drew it out of the envelope.

'Mavourneen,' he sneered, as he handed it over. 'She would give herself a fancy name! And she knows full well I can't stand her with her eyes done up like a tart. Must have taken hours, tricking herself up. And the brooch I gave her! Chose it herself and it cost me all of ten pounds at that pawnbrokers in Oxford Street. "What do you want a fancy thing like that for?" I says . . .' Once again Millage nearly wept.

'I don't want to discourage you, Mr Millage,' Nat remarked as he studied the photograph, 'but you're asking for trouble when you take on a wife who looks like that.'

He sprang to his feet and thrust his face close to Nat's. 'You're wrong. You don't know my Val, she's a good girl at heart.'

'Don't let's argue,' Nat returned, 'but I really cannot see how the fact of the name York on a photograph can lead you to think that you have any clue as to the murderer of York Cragg.'

'Look, I want my wife back a lot more than I want this here reward, but I reckon if I had this five thou she'd come back a lot quicker. I'd give her a good hiding, I'd sweeten her up with the money, and we'd start afresh. Women like a good hiding; if I'd done it sooner I reckon I'd have been all right.'

Nat was getting a little tired of Mr Millage's matrimonial troubles. Briskly he swept them aside and asked for details of the meeting with Sir Jason Cragg.

And so they learned that Jason had driven to the factory on the Great North Road in his Rolls-Royce and had asked to see Ernest Millage in the middle of the afternoon, and he and Ernest had talked together for half an hour, outside, standing by the old car in full view of all the office. And he, Ernest, had been so upset he'd packed up the afternoon's work and gone home to talk it over with his mother, who had advised him to do nothing for the moment. Leave it to father Cragg, she had said. He's got all the money behind him, he'll find her. He was a big businessman, used to getting things done; Mrs Millage senior was in no doubt at all that the wretched Valentine would soon be brought home repenting.

'But what could you think York Cragg had to do with her? He was a happily married man, living here.'

Ernest Millage shook his head firmly. 'He led a double life is my guess. He enticed my Valentine and he's set her up in a little establishment.'

'Look, you've been reading some cheap fiction, Mr Millage. Things don't happen like that nowadays. But suppose he had . . . what would it have to do with his murder, unless, of course, you killed him?'

'Me?' Millage's mouth all but dropped open. 'Me?'

'Surely you can see what you've presented us with this evening? One great big motive; motive, Mr Millage. Motive is one of the things the police are looking for.'

'Police!'

'Ever heard of them?'

Millage looked as though someone had stamped on him.

'One big omission, however . . . you haven't given us a motive for killing Sir Jason, so far. Perhaps you could tell us a little more, Mr Millage?'

A curious metamorphosis had crept over Nat, an air of firm authority that caused Mr Millage to quail.

'There's a lot you haven't told us, Mr Millage. I should like to know, word for word, what exactly passed between you and Sir Jason that day outside the factory. Come now, we've only got half the story.'

'On my honour . . . !' he began to protest and then, under Nat's firm look, he changed into a lower gear. He slumped down with his hands hanging between his knees and went into a long narrative full of 'he says to me' and 'I says to him' and 'he says' and 'I says, I says', from which a fairly accurate picture emerged.

Sir Jason had wasted no time but had at once brought out several copies of a photograph. 'Is this your wife?' he had asked. And 'Is this her handwriting?' And Millage had said that it was neither his wife as he knew her nor her handwriting as he knew it. He was exceedingly angry, to begin with. Sir Jason had told him to calm down, nothing was to be gained by spluttering with anger. It was, was it not, in fact, a photograph of his wife and the loving message was one which his wife would be capable of writing? Yes, Millage had reluctantly admitted it. The name 'Mavourneen' was not one by which her husband knew her, but it was at least within the bounds of possibility that she would give herself such a name for the exclusive use of a lover. Millage had to admit this, too.

Then Sir Jason had asked a lot of questions the half of which Millage couldn't for the life of him remember. He had asked what sort of acting parts had she had, and here Millage had been forced to admit that she wasn't so much an actress as a singer and dancer. 'In the chorus, in fact?' Sir Jason had summed up. He also made Millage admit that she had not, in actual fact, ever appeared on any London stage; her appearances had been mainly in the provinces, the smaller towns: Grimsby, Ashby-de-la-Zouche, Wigan. 'A touring company?' Yes, touring companies, when she was doing well, but she didn't always do well, she spent a lot of time in the agencies. The stage was a very poorly paid profession when you reckoned how much time they spent unemployed.

How long had Millage known her before marriage? Four weeks, to be precise. That wasn't very long, was it? How was Millage to be sure that she had broken with all her old connections? Alas, he wasn't. He only knew he loved her, and she loved him, and he had believed that she wanted security. Then she might have been York Cragg's mistress for years before Millage knew her? Quite so. Could it be that York Cragg had tired of her and she continued to love him? No, Millage was quite definite there; that was absolutely out of the question. But still, Sir Jason had persisted, she had run away from him. Had Millage been expecting that? He had not; it was the shock of his life when he found she'd gone, gone without a word, without a trace.

'Perhaps she's dead. Murdered too,' Sir Jason had said.

Millage had been deeply shocked at that; he also considered it completely impossible until Sir Jason reminded him that his own son, York, had been murdered most foully and that such things did happen, almost every day. His wife had vanished without leaving any hint as to where she was going, and from then, last November was it, until now he had had no sign at all that she still existed. How could he state definitely that she was not dead?

And then: 'Did you report her disappearance, Millage?' No, he had not.

'Why?'

Why? Why? WHY?

Because he, Millage, did not want everybody to know that his wife had run away from him.

'What a putrid reason!' Sir Jason had said.

But it wasn't really. Respectability, the step-sister and a poor relation of pride, was something that Millage and his like treasured more than any other thing. In his halting way Millage had tried to explain this, but it was something Sir Jason was quite unable to understand. He, Jason, did not give a damn what anyone thought of him, and he couldn't understand that anyone else could.

It was obvious at this stage, to Nat, and possibly to Easter, that Sir Jason was convinced that Ernest Millage had killed his wife and either hidden, or disposed of, the body, and, as a natural corollary, had also stabbed York, whose suspicions with regard to the husband of his late mistress had been thoroughly aroused.

'And so I says to him: "What are you going to do, sir?"' Millage went on. 'And he says: "Find your wife, Millage, either dead or alive." And I says: "Can I have one of these photos?" and he says: "Take it, by all means." I wanted to show it to Mum; she'd never have believed it if she hadn't seen it with her own eyes. "I'll get in touch with you," he says, "possibly tomorrow. I want to think this thing over." He thanked me and says ta ta! and that was the last I saw of him. Next day but one I read about him being found, here, it would be.' Millage stared in some horror at the comfortable-looking hearth. 'In this very room,' he repeated in wonder.

CHAPTER VII

For an hour Millage 'chewed the rag' as Nat put it; ruminating, speculating, reminiscing, discoursing, debating; the fire burned low and it was only when Easter rose to make it up that he showed signs of leaving.

'What was your wife's stage name?'

Millage looked even more unhappy. 'That's just it! She's had half a dozen that I know of. She went on the stage as a kiddy of twelve in pantomime and I reckon that was what spoiled her; she got the idea that she was good and that one day, if she tried hard enough, she'd have her name in lights across Piccadilly Circus for certain. She started as "Kitty Valentine", that I do know, and when we met she was –' Mr Millage cleared his throat in slight embarrassment – 'she was one of these here stationary nudes at Collin's Music Hall, in Islington. Lucy de Lacy, she called herself then, but she'd no pride in it, a stop-gap, she called it, and when she packed it up there she stepped out of the name.'

'Like she stepped out of her clothes,' Nat murmured.

'Pardon?'

'Where did she get her stage names?'

'Thought them up –' Mr Millage smiled – 'talk about imagination! That's why it didn't surprise me when I saw the loving message: "To my darling York; your Mavourneen".' The smile dissolved in bitterness. 'Sloppy . . .' In exasperation, Millage jumped to his feet, wrapping his gaudy coat around him and tying the sash belt.

Nat was still holding the photograph. 'One thing,' he said, 'I must ask you. Don't waste any more time before informing the police that your wife is missing. You've made a big mistake in not getting in touch with them up to now.

And if I were you, I'd keep quiet about your York Cragg ideas.'

Millage's eyes narrowed suspiciously. 'You would, would you? I'll see about that.'

'Just as you please, of course.' Nat shrugged. 'But one thing I must ask you, as a favour. May I keep this photograph for a day or two?'

'If I'm to go to the police to tell them my wife's missing, I'd best take it, that stands to reason.'

'Haven't you any others?'

'Dozens of 'em, literally dozens. She was always having them took, for agents and managers and so on.'

'Well, take as many as you like to the police; but remember, if you take this particular one, they will want to know all about that inscription, "to my darling York", whether you've made up your mind to tell them or not. I only want to help you, Millage. And I don't want to raise your hopes, in any way, and have to disappoint you; but if you could lend me this photograph for a day or so, I'd be grateful.'

Easter held out her hand for it and studied it as Mr Millage collected himself for departure.

Out in the hall, Millage whispered something to Nat, who showed him into the cloakroom; when he came out, Nat was staring out into the dark of the drive; he had turned out the hall light and the threshold was now illuminated only from the light of the sitting-room.

'Well, good night,' Millage managed a 'Sir' at last. He shook hands. 'Thanks for . . . thanks . . .' he stumbled out into the dark.

'Haven't you a torch?'

Millage said no.

'Well, look, over there are the lights of the main road; there are buses up to midnight so you'll be all right. Turn right round that clump of bushes and you'll see the lights ahead. So long.'

'You've got my address OK?'
'Yes, I have. Good night, Millage.'
'G'night, sir.'

Nat waited, listening to the sound of his receding footsteps before closing the door. He returned to the sitting-room where the fire was now burning brightly.

'I didn't turn on the outside light and his step was a bit uncertain. I may be wrong, of course, but one didn't get the impression that he'd been here before and knew his way about. And his hand-shake was firm and warm, unlike that of a dead fish. And did he ask to go to the lavatory for purely natural reasons or . . . ? What are you burning, Easter, what the hell are you burning? Oh, you bloody little silly fool. Oh, damn you, damn you!'

'I had to.'

He took her by the shoulders and shook her, shouting angrily: 'You utter fool!' But he might as well have tried to shake a female puma; she fought back, scratching and biting and making vicious jabs with her knee until, in self-defence, he took a Japanese hold of her and flipped her face downwards on to the sofa. After which he was as emptied of anger as the top half of an hour-glass is emptied of sand and, feeling slightly foolish, he adjusted his tie and collar and pulled down his cuffs to a nice proportion below his sleeves.

For some minutes she lay, as she had fallen, vibrating. Nat took the empty tumblers into the kitchen, where he rinsed them under the hot tap and dried them carefully. He opened the table drawer where some of Easter's *batterie de cuisine* lay in a tidy row, and took out the sheet of paper, tearing it into small pieces which he put into his pocket. He took the tumblers back into the sitting-room and laid them on the tray.

Fragments of burnt photograph were wafting lightly about in a black corner of the fire; a faintish green flame flickered in and out on the surface where the photograph had been. But the picture of the woman was etched deeply upon his mind's eye.

Easter uncoiled herself slowly, pushed her hair out of her eyes, and blew her nose.

'Why did you burn it?'

'You know perfectly well why.'

'Self-respect,' he said derisively, 'exactly like Ernest Millage. You don't want the world to know you're a wronged woman. You little bourgeois!'

'Take that view if you want. It could have been altruistic. I took the two copies out of Jason's case, after he was dead. His despatch-case was on the hall table for hours and the photographs were in it, together with the negative he had made. He gave me back the original photograph, so I burned the lot. It's much better so. That photograph has done, I mean might do, endless harm.'

There was nothing unusual in her composure. Women, Nathaniel knew, were like that. Fighting like wild cats, screaming, hysterical, beyond themselves one moment . . . and the next . . . powdering their noses and applying lipstick as though nothing had happened. Feeling, in fact, a lot better, whilst their pulverized males could only gape in an astonishment which was in no way mitigated by the number of times it was experienced.

She was like a small Siamese kitten which, having ripped a pair of Dior nylons to mere threads, sits back on its haunches and looks up wide-eyed; infinitely, deliciously, free from moral wrong.

'You look absolute heaven like that,' Nathaniel said disapprovingly, and, gathering her up into a silken armful, he kissed her crushingly. 'I loathe you,' he murmured passionately, 'you horrid, common, screaming little hellcat.'

CHAPTER VIII

'But nevertheless . . .' Nathaniel scraped away at his face with his cut-throat razor, the use of which he took some pride in. 'Be that as it may . . .' and 'However . . .'

All that had been parenthesis and had nothing to do with the matter in hand. Besides, it hadn't come to anything. He had carried her upstairs and had tossed her down on her bed and left her there. He had turned out the lights before leaving and had locked the front door after him, putting the mortice key back into the house through the letter-box.

And now he was going to get into the old Rolls-Royce and drive madly about until he found 'Mavourneen' and he was going to leave Easter to think it over. Because he was seriously annoyed with her. It was all very well, but to destroy so finally something which might have shed some light at least upon York Cragg's private life, and thus, possibly, upon his murder, seemed quixotic to the point of sheer insanity. Furthermore, he did not trust Easter as a pursuant of lofty but impracticable ideas; she was as likely to have done it from self-interest as from devotion to her dead husband's reputation.

She didn't know anything about Nathaniel Sapperton if she thought that mere destruction of the photographs was going to discourage him. On the contrary, it only hardened his resolve to find 'Mavourneen' with the pixie ears and the lovely pouting mouth. If, of course, she was still alive.

Ernest Millage could have murdered her and buried her in the small back garden at Rosedale, Edgware, in the county of Middlesex. Anyone could be a murderer and, unless one knew without a shadow of doubt, it was impossible to say for certain: he is a murderer; *or*: he is not a murderer. And moreover, Nathaniel reminded himself, how much nearer to being a murderer was he himself when he wished somebody out of the way, than the man who raised his fist and, knocking down this same somebody, accidentally killed him. The term *murderer* needed revising; it was losing its meaning.

Nathaniel dabbed his face with shaving lotion.

Ernest Millage might have murdered all three but, if he had, he was pretty sure of himself; he would keep until Nathaniel had made some further investigations. One thing Nat was certain of was that Millage wouldn't shoot himself to avoid punishment; he was the type who would face it, cocky and self-confident to the last. The tears which had so nearly overflowed down Millage's face had been those of sympathy for his own heart-breaking situation, rather than any sign of remorse.

And another thing. Mrs Valentine Millage would read at least one newspaper, provided she was alive. Would she be able to resist the dangling bait of Five Thousand Pounds? From what he had heard of her, she would leap at the reward like a trout at a piece of orange-peel, only too eager to come over with excessive detail about her love-affair with York Cragg. Would she take the unusual step of getting in touch with the widow? No, that was something that Ernest Millage did for special, personal reasons. Mrs Valentine Millage would communicate with the police. Or not. And if not – she was dead.

CHAPTER IX

Having ascertained at a police station which was the right directory in which to look up the information he required, he made a list of the theatrical agents in London. There was a surprising number of them and there was nothing to indicate which were the reputable ones and which were not. In any case, what did it matter?

It was slow, tiring work; most of them seemed to be situated on top floors, requiring the mounting of innumerable steep narrow stairways. There were others in basements and some over shops with obscure entrances round the back. If he had pictured himself picking his way through a galaxy of glamorous starlets, reality fell far short of his hopes.

At the bigger, better agents, there were small groups of people waiting who, from their appearance, might well have been people waiting in an out-patients' waiting-hall. Occasionally, someone outstanding would catch the eye: a couple of tiny gnomes, waiting for a circus engagement; a coloured girl six feet tall with measurements 50-23-39, dressed in tight tartan trews and a sequin-encrusted sweater; an elderly Negro with snow-white hair, like white icing on a chocolate cake; a child of ten with white-blonde, candy-floss hair and huge black eyes, like an illustration out of *The Wide, Wide World*. But they all wore the dull, uniform expression of people who wait, without much hope.

Nearly always Mr Sticklebaum, Mr Pfui and Mr Glamer and their brethren were out, leaving the office in charge of a single woman, elderly more often than not.

Each time Nathaniel trotted out his piece, it seemed to him more phoney: 'I'm looking for someone called Valentine Millage, or you may know her as Lucy de Lacy or Kitty Valentine. Would you be good enough to see if she is on your files?'

He suffered considerably from his sympathetic manner which nearly always involved the need to appear to listen attentively to chatter about last week's influenza which kept her at home in bed so that she still wasn't feeling up to the mark; the misfortune which had occurred to a pair of glasses that morning as she left the house; the annoyance of not being able to have her luncheon hour from twelve to one at the same time as her boy-friend; the peculiarities of the office cat!

But the time wasted was repaid because, when nothing turned up under any of the three names he mentioned, he asked if he might look through the photograph files and, having shown himself to be pleasant, he received co-operation in return.

At the eleventh visit he had some success. Under the heading 'Miscellaneous', Lucy de Lacy (nude) was filed, the form being pinned to two others which described her as 'Kitty Valentine' (song and dance) and 'Veronica Valentine' (show girl). There were also three photographs of an extraordinary variety: full-length, she was wearing a bikini of sequins, her hair fluffed out into a dark cloud; in the second she was in some sort of Russian outfit, her hair hanging in two plaits on either side of her face, and in the third she stood in a haughty pose in a skin-tight evening frock, but in each it was the unmistakable face of 'Mavourneen'.

What an old-fashioned type York Cragg must have been at heart, Nathaniel mused: in these days, when any number of young women could be had for a few cocktails and the asking, why complicate one's life with a woman of this sort, like a roguish Edwardian masher? It was incredible but, as Nathaniel's Lancashire grandmother so often said in the dialect: 'There's nowt so queer as folk!'

'When did you last see her?'

'It was last September she was in. As a matter of fact she got herself fixed up through another agent.' The clerk shuffled the papers about for a minute before saying: 'Yes, I thought so. I've made a note of it. There was a postcard from her on the seventh of the tenth of last fall, asking us to keep her name on our books; she'd got fixed up temporary.'

'Where?'

'Ah, there you're asking me!'

'Do you mean to say you don't know!' Nathaniel exclaimed, incredulous with frustration.

The clerk, too, was disappointed; he had seemed so nice, very much a gentleman.

'As a matter of fact,' she said coldly, 'I do. Or rather, I happen to know the agents who fixed her up: Obergurgle in Long Acre.'

'How clever of you to remember,' Nathaniel gushed a little retardedly.

'A little birdie told me,' she said severely. 'Shut the door on your way out!'

'Music hall's done for,' Mr Obergurgle lisped nostalgically. 'The young folk have no time for it; the only audience they collect is a handful of old grampars. They don't want a good laugh, when they go out, this generation don't; they're a lot of culture cretins in their drains and drapes ... ah me!' He explored the inside of his nose thoughtfully. 'This lot is touring the provinces under Wulfie Lyon; it's a re-hash of the show he had on Clacton Pier last summer, only not near so good. And this 'ere, what's her name?' He peered through the lower-half of his steamy bi-focals, at the engagement book: 'Wanda Valentine ...'

'Veronica Valentine,' Nat murmured. 'Have you seen her?' His voice took on a hoarse note arising from excitement.

'Yes, I've seen her,' Mr Obergurgle said dully, but he was more interested in his nose; he made no comment whatever. 'I can't say where you'll find them now but here's a list of places with theatres that put on shows like Wulfie Lyon's.' After some rummaging in drawers and files he produced a copy of a typewritten list. 'It's all there. Rochdale, Halifax, Huddersfield, Newcastle ... Happy landings,' he said sarcastically. 'If I had a break, I'd prefer Majorca meself.'

So would Nat, but at the moment there was, unfortunately, no choice.

The Third Part

CHAPTER I

He did not telephone to Easter before leaving. To do so would mean that he would be obliged to say when he would be back; he might be back in twenty-four hours, and he might be back in ten days. He did not want to have to say. Nor did he want to give any explanation for his absence; it would do Easter good, after her exhibition of temper, to cool off slowly; it might make her realize that she had behaved, to say the least of it, foolishly.

Nathaniel was delighted with his newly-purchased car. Up to the present he had had little time to fuss over her, but the mere fact of possession gave him infinite satisfaction. She was not yet a veteran but she had the dignity that a veteran did not possess; she engendered admiration rather than ribaldry. A drop-head coupé, she had a leather hood which worked on the principle of a perambulator hood; Jason had had it kept supple with repeated dressings of saddle soap. Two butterfly screws secured it to the windscreen and, when they were loosened, the hood could be pushed upright, slipping back and collapsing with slow dignity, fold on fold, above the boot.

On the door was a coat of arms, a paschal-lamb, inappropriately enough, with crossed oars behind it: the badge of the Golden Fleece Shipping Company. The radiator cap had the Rolls's silver lady fixed to it, that derivation from the Winged Victory of Samothrace, standing, as in all the old models, and on the front of the radiator the over-lapping capital R's were red, showing that it was built before the death of Sir Henry Royce.

A weighty T-shaped carriage key for the boot was kept

in one of the door pockets, and over each keyhole, on either side of the boot, heavy metal caps clipped down to prevent rain entering. The lid of the boot opened upwards into a great rubber-lined cave; it was kept open by two metal elbows. Nathaniel slung his canvas grip containing his night things inside and re-locked the boot, though this was hardly necessary as the lid kept down by its own weight. The number plate was a solid metal job and hung, like a dangling petticoat, below the boot, stating its owner to be 'PP3'. The only tribute to progress that had been made was the electrification of the cut-glass oil lamps used as parking lights on either side of the windscreen, and the two automatic rear lights fixed to the great swooping mudguards at the rear.

'To the North,' the road signs said, giving Nathaniel a small thrill that was wholly unconnected with reality. But Dick Turpin made better time; hours later, having achieved Doncaster, half asphixiated, Nathaniel told himself that he had had enough, for the moment, of the stinking alley that was the Great North Road; he went to bed at the first likely hostelry he could find.

CHAPTER II

A telephone call between the Ramsgates and Easter Cragg was an almost daily occurrence. Often for as long as a quarter of an hour, the two women chatted about their plans for the day and the events of the previous day. Easter had made slightly amused references to a 'boy-friend' with whom she had dined several times of late.

Jill had said to her husband: 'You know, I believe Easter's beginning to get over everything; there's a man of sorts about.'

'Good,' her husband had answered, 'it's the very best

thing that could happen from everybody's point of view. Easter could become quite a liability.'

'I'll be very tactful; I won't ask her about it.'

'No, don't. We'll be asked to meet him if there's anything in it.'

Consequently, Jill chattered on about her own affairs and did not ask Easter questions. She talked about the children, one of whom was in his first term at a kindergarten school; her new suit; the film they had seen the previous evening at the Curzon; their plans for the summer holidays abroad. And then she said:

'Oh, by the way. John saw Jason's old car yesterday. He was lunching at the Traveller's Club and he saw it parked outside in the square when he went in. When he came out two hours later it was still there, but, whilst John was backing out our own car, the new owner of the Rolls came to collect it. And who do you think has bought it?'

Silence.

'Ian Wainwright.'

Still silence.

'Of course, you've never met him. He's been in the Middle East for the last two years, but you've heard York and Jason speak of him. He's a very bright lad indeed. He was decorated for some terrific thing he did in the Secret Service during the War, and now he's attached to the Foreign Office on the very hush-hush side. Are you still there, Easter?'

'Yes.' Pause. 'I'm still here.'

'Are you getting a cold, darling? Your voice sounds awfully hoarse.'

'Perhaps I am. This Ian Wainwright – of course, Jason and York often spoke of him. He sent us a cheque for a wedding present.'

'Well, he's home for a bit now, waiting for a new posting. He was in England and saw Jason just before ... he's been in Sweden since then; his family are on holiday there with his wife's people. My dear, he's got the most glamorous Swedish wife! What did you say, Easter?'

'He has children?'

'Two! They look absolute popsies, John says, from their photographs. Both very fair. Well, it isn't quite a coincidence Ian's buying Jason's old car. He wrote to the solicitor and asked if he could. We're so pleased about it; I don't like to think of Jason's dear old car knocking about, belonging to anyone, do you?'

'Jill . . .'

'Yes, darling?'

'What's this Ian Wainwright like, to look at, I mean?'

'You must meet him. John asked him to dine but he's away on business for the next few weeks. He'll let us know when he's back.'

'But what does he *look* like?'

'Nothing much to look at. But you'd like him. He's amusing.'

'Where's he *living*?'

'They haven't a permanent home. He's probably in an hotel. Now, what are you doing today? It's going to be heavenly. It's Nanny's day out; come over after lunch and go for a walk with us on the Heath. No? Well, perhaps you ought to look after that cold.'

Easter put down the receiver and went to look at her reflection in the looking-glass. She stared at herself in astonishment as though she was surprised to see the same creature she had been some quarter of an hour earlier.

She sat down and turned over the pages of the new magazine which had been delivered that morning. It was one of her favourite magazines but she was not interested. She jumped up and went out into the yard, looking up at the block of flats and in particular at the window she knew to be Nathaniel Sapperton's bedroom. It was closed. She went to the telephone and dialled the number of his flat.

'Is that Mr Ian Wainwright?' she would ask.

Prr-prr, pause, prr-prr, pause, prr-prr, prr-prr.

It was like toothache, each ringing sound stabbing deep into her nerves. There was a certain grim satisfaction in the self-torture, which helped to make bearable the agonizing doubt and uncertainty into which Jill's scrap of gossip had plunged her.

At hourly intervals throughout the day and most of the night she dialled and listened for several minutes to the bell ringing in the empty flat before replacing the receiver. Sooner or later he would answer; he could hardly have gone away without saying a word to her.

But no light appeared in his room nor was there any change in the position of the curtains.

He had come into her life like a great moth, blundering in at dusk; he had beaten up the settling dust of her life as the big moth disturbs the fluff on the electric light bulb. And Easter, because she was lonely, had accepted him, believed everything he told her, trusted him. She had not questioned his obvious desire to help and comfort her. As an attractive, solitary young woman, what was more natural than that he should seek her out? Oh, the vanity of it! If Easter was angry it was with herself, that clever, detached self upon whom she relied utterly. If that safe self could fail her, what else might not fail? This so-called Nathaniel Sapperton might murder her; Easter winced when she thought of the hours they had spent together, and alone.

She looked in the looking-glass, reproachfully seeking, in her own well-known, well-beloved face, the answer to the question: how could she have forgotten herself to such an extent? But there was no sly pixie looking from her eyes; her face was smooth and kitten-innocent, slightly puffy and expressionless, showing nothing of the troubles through which she had recently come. A baby-face with wide guileless eyes and the mouth that seemed to pout for kisses; it told her nothing but looked back at her in mild surprise.

To dial, to press the receiver to her ear and to listen to the monotonous *prr-prr* became a habit; there was nothing else she could do.

CHAPTER III

Mrs Sam Bacon was far more excited about the Five Thousand Pounds reward than she would have cared to admit; though she went about her housework as usual, she was seething with sensationalism inside. She hung the front page of the *Daily Gape*, with its tall headlines proclaiming the reward, from the chimneypiece, and throughout the following day her eyes turned to it again and again.

Doris Bacon was a great go-er-in for competitions; upon one occasion she had won a musquash coat for her selection of coats in order of merit in a Sunday paper. Once she had won a cake for guessing its weight, and another time she had gained a bottle of whisky for guessing the correct number of beans in a jar. It was, of course, over-ambitious to the point of farce to imagine that she could win the Five Thousand Pounds reward but someone could. Some quite ordinary person would win it. Someone, possibly, like themselves. Because, of course, there was an answer.

It might be that the answer would never be discovered and that the Five Thousand would lie unclaimed but that didn't mean that no answer existed. Sir Jason Cragg and his son York had been killed, there was no denying that, and therefore someone had killed them, since they had neither killed themselves nor been killed by accident.

Sam had been right in on the whole thing from as early a moment as possible, but somehow, Mrs Bacon sighed heavily, Sam's mind, somehow . . . but Mrs Bacon would not allow herself to think disloyally. There was nothing wrong with Sam's mind; he was a good, reliable policeman and she was proud of him. It wouldn't do for a policeman to go off at a tangent, wondering . . .

But there was no harm in a policeman's wife doing a bit of thinking. In the dresser drawer lay the copies of the *Daily Gape* in which had appeared the reports of the police-court proceedings to date, of both murders. Mrs Bacon, leaning across the table, studied them carefully. They told you nothing, really, she speculated. Little bits of sensationalism and sentimentalism were picked out and enlarged upon by the *Daily Gape*'s own reporter, who was like someone picking the roasted almonds off the top of a rich fruit cake. On an old postcard she jotted down the dates upon which the reports appeared and on her way back from the shops, armed with her laden shopping basket, she turned in at the public library.

In the reading-room she whispered to the attendant: 'Could I please see the back numbers of —' having been told, by way of several large posters that: 'Top People Read *The Times*', Mrs Bacon felt she could go no higher — '*The Times!*' she hissed and, putting her shopping basket down carefully, so that she would not break the eggs, Mrs Bacon brought her reading-glasses out of her pocket and gave them a good polish with her pocket handkerchief and breath.

CHAPTER IV

People were kind, and ready to be helpful. Nowhere in Asia, or, for that matter, in Southern Europe, would it be possible to go about asking for a theatrical company travelling under the aegis of someone with a ridiculous zoological name without giving some explanation. But in the North of England, at least, they answered his queries with grave courtesy, and if they felt eaten up with curiosity they did not show it. Mr Sapperton discovered that by telephoning to an office in Manchester he would be told exactly where the Wulfie Lyon show was playing. And this he did.

Having been born and brought up in the County Palatine of Lancaster he was pleased to learn that they were at present playing the Pier Pavilion at Liverton-upon-Sands under the name of 'Yours Cheerfully'.

It was early afternoon when he arrived there and, having had no difficulty in getting a room at the Empire Hotel, he left his bag and the car and sauntered out on to the 'Front'.

An icy wind from the north-west seemed to have blown most human beings from the tarmac, but there were people huddled in the landward sides of the shelters. As far as it was possible to see, one saw grey sand, stretching out, flat and uneventful, into infinity, beyond which, Nathaniel knew, the sea was coming in at the rate of something like five miles per hour. It was a busy sea, covering miles upon miles of grey sand twice a day, a sea so worn out by activity that, when it arrived at the 'Front', it would have lost its sea-savour and would both taste and look like icy-cold, diluted pea-soup.

The pier strode out across the sands, its long iron legs looking strangely bare from a distance. The Pavilion was at the entrance to the pier; the box office was open and, with his heart beginning to thud a little from excitement, Mr Sapperton stepped into the foyer and looked eagerly round for the photographs of the cast. But there were none, only a notice-board bearing the names of the performers which he studied, with increasing disappointment, for several minutes.

'Wulfie Lyon,' he read, 'offers something for everybody.'

'YOURS CHEERFULLY!'
'New Faces — New Ideas — New Acts.'

It was all rather puzzling; amongst some thirty or so names on the bill that of Veronica Valentine did not appear. She might, of course, be one of *The Tophole Trio*, or part of *Gloria Gagg and her Girlies*, one of the pawns in *The Crooning Checks*. Was it possible that she was a unit in *Moon and Son*?

Deeply reflective he became aware that the young lady in the box office was regarding him with as much curiosity as he was devoting to the notices.

'One stall for the first house,' he said, putting down ten shillings.

'Twice nightly on Wednesdays and Saturdays only,' she said firmly. 'Tonight at seven.'

'One stall,' he repeated.

'One...' she pronounced it to rhyme with on, 'three and six, please.'

'Do you happen to know if there is someone called Veronica Valentine playing?' he asked politely.

She shook her head. 'I wouldn't know. They're only here for a week. They're good, though. That Tommy Raffles is a scream!'

Thoughtfully, Nathaniel paced the damp boards of the pier. In the season, the pier was a seething mass of people, all, apparently, enjoying themselves. But at the moment he had it to himself. When he was a small boy, he remembered, he had had a tremendous thrill from looking down between the cracks of the boards, at the sea miles and miles below. But today his diversion held neither thrill nor attraction. The Ghost Train was closed down, the Amusement Palace was closed, and even the kiosk selling rock, toffee apples and Phulnana cachous was shrouded in tarpaulin. When he was young, there had been machines all along the pier in which one could, by inserting a penny, have exciting competitions with oneself, trying to catch worthless articles with giant clippers, playing a football match and enjoying What the Butler Saw. But all these attractions had been either banished altogether or were now gathered under the roof of the Amusement Palace where an attendant could keep a watchful eye to see that young toughs did not bust them wide open.

It was eight degrees below dull.

He returned to tea at the Empire Hotel, where he sat suffering acutely under the curious glances of old ladies who tried to look as though they were engrossed in their library books. Dinner, he noticed, was at seven, the same time as 'Yours Cheerfully' began, making it quite evident that those who dined at seven did not go to variety shows on the pier. So he would have to go without dinner. But if the entertainment started at seven it would be over by ten, at the latest, more likely by nine-thirty. He might find a chop house open to which he could take 'Veronica Valentine' to eat 'after the show'.

He had a definite plan of action; he would send round a note and ask her to meet him afterwards; he would be the Unknown Admirer, struck all of a heap. He did not anticipate much trouble in persuading her at least to have supper with him. What happened after that would depend upon what he was able to discover during the meal. So far everything had gone splendidly; he had had marvellous luck. It had been only a fifty-fifty chance that Mr Millage's runaway wife had returned to the stage; Nathaniel quailed at the thought of the time he might have spent ascertaining this; two days of traipsing round the agents had been more than enough. And now, he was going to see her at last; the fabulous *Mavourneen*, that seducer of strong men and breaker-up of the happiest of homes . . . he looked at his watch: still two hours to go. He drifted out into the grey evening and sought cheerful companionship at the Dun Cow.

CHAPTER V

There was nothing bucolic about the clientele of the Dun Cow. By the time he had absorbed three pints of mild and bitter, for one only of which he was allowed to pay, he began almost to feel for the straws in his own hair. Their comment upon current affairs was voluble and astringent. They were much-travelled, too. The man in the cloth cap, a leather worker, had just returned with his wife and two 'kiddies' from an Easter holiday in Taormina; the man who was clearly a bookie had spent his Easter in Paris and from the smacking of his lips one gathered that he had split Montmartre wide open; the man with the beautifully-cut trousers and the suede short boots, to which he proudly referred as 'brothel-creepers', was planning a holiday in Jugoslavia on the proceeds of property sales, and the tiny man who had nipped in from the greengrocer's next door squeaked that he was off to Le Touquet for a golfing weekend.

Far from being the back o'beyond, Liverton-upon-Sands was clearly only a little short of the centre of the universe; Nathaniel felt proud to be there and sure of the success of his venture. He stood everybody a round of drinks, including the landlord.

' 'Ere's your very good 'ealth.' Down south the landlord would undoubtedly have added, with the utmost casualness: 'Staying long?' It may, of course, have been in part due to the flat vowels with which Nathaniel lightly larded his speech that he was accepted as one of themselves.

At ten to seven, when he made known that it was time for him to go, he told them he was on his way to the Pier Pavilion; the announcement was accepted as normal, no one even smiled. Each made his own particular casual gesture of farewell.

Outside it was not yet dark, the time having been recently advanced an hour. The sky was a lowering grey and the lights of the Pier Pavilion stood out with weird effect. Nathaniel bought his programme and subsided into his seat with a thrill of excitement that had more to do with the overture which the small orchestra was playing than with the beer he had consumed. There was a certain quality about the playing of the orchestra which engendered an excitement which he had not felt for many years. He studied the screen, plastered with advertisements and peculiar to variety shows from time immemorial; he looked round; the auditorium was filling up rapidly and for the most part, he noticed, with men.

When the curtain went up he realized, almost at once, that variety was not, as Mr Obergurgle appeared to believe, on the way out. It was, in fact, very much alive. There was nothing whatever that was 'new', as the poster declared; it was as old as music hall itself: the same old thing, the mixture as before, but each item was received with a storm of clapping and after particular favourites there were shrill whistles and cat-calls.

There were no less than six comedians, ranging from the arch-face-puller down through the smile-less lunatic, the drunken Irishman, the comic who fired off jokes like a tommy-gun, the lewd-looking fellow in the top hat who left almost everything to the minds of his audience, to the last, lowest and best of all, the coster's own comic, a delightful individual with no talent whatever but with a tremendous personality. His appearance was greeted with a thunder of applause; he wore a cloth cap and short dress trousers showing red and white striped football stockings, and a tail-coat several sizes too large for him with a red button which wouldn't keep buttoned for as long as you could count three. The lights went green as he came on and, when he stated gloomily that he was going mouldy, the women in the audience screamed with the same delight they might feel on the giant racer in the amusement park. He brought the genuine antiques out of the joke box, one after another: 'Are you 'andcuffed?' he asked, suggesting that the applause was below standard. 'Ladies and gentlemen, you will observe that during this wonderful dance I am now doing, my feet have not once left my body!' and Nathaniel, along with everyone else, roared with laughter.

It was all rather a long way from Jason and York Cragg and his pleasure had, of course, a lot to do with the alcohol now coursing round in his bloodstream, but for the moment Nathaniel abandoned himself to pleasure.

It was only during the equilibrium act at the end, which was done by three young people obviously under fifteen, that Nathaniel realized there had been no chorus, no nudes and no display of rhythmic legs. Fed on *Reveille* and the *Daily Mirror*, people no longer needed to go to the theatre to see glorious bodies. During 'God Save the Queen' he studied the programme feverishly: *the woman lassoist, Big Chief, the Human Candelabra, the Sixteen Singing Schoolboys*...

With something like a feeling of panic, he realized that Mr Millage's Val did not appear in the programme under any of her stage names. Who was he looking for? he thought dizzily. But what did it matter? He would know that fabulous face anywhere.

'Is this the face that launched a thousand ships?' he asked himself as he went round the back to the stage door, wavering very slightly. His watch said nine-fifteen, so there was still time to go back to his friends at the Dun Cow. Something had gone wrong somewhere: he had never thought seriously that she existed, Nathaniel now told himself. Tomorrow there would be time enough to think everything out.

There wasn't a porter at the stage door; peering inside he heard a good deal of noise; talking, even shouting. He retreated hastily and walked some yards to the railing at the side of the pier, against which he leaned, hands stuffed deeply into the pockets of his British warm. The sea had come in and was making no great fuss on the sands below, the wind was whining through the ornamental ironwork of the pier; he waited until the first member of the cast came out, but he waited impatiently, sure, now, that he would be unsuccessful and only anxious to see if the landlord of the Dun Cow could produce some food.

'Do you happen to know if there is a Veronica Valentine in the show?' he asked. *The Sixteen Schoolboys* had come tumbling out as noisily uninhibited as a pack of choirboys out of church. None of them had the least idea until a small one piped: 'Miss Valentine, that's Minnehaha; I had to take somepin to the "Forty-Eight-Hour" cleaners for her this morning.'

'Tell her there's someone to see her, there's a good lad.' Nathaniel pressed half a crown into his hand and, taking the programme out of his pocket, he tried to study it once again, in the poor light from the stage door.

'*Big Chief, the Human Candelabra*', and below, in much smaller print: '*and Minnehaha*'.

Minnehaha being the squaw who had handed the great Big Chief his torches of burning petrol to swallow! She had had straight black hair and a reddish brown face and she had worn trousers edged with feathers and a hair-band straight across her brow in which one feather was standing upright.

The small boy returned, looking at him for a moment oddly, as though sizing him up. Apparently he liked what he saw, for he approached and said in a low voice: 'She's not having any.'

'What do you mean?'

'Big Chief scares the lights out of her. She's hopping it out the main entrance.'

She was, was she?

The front entrance of the Pavilion was flush with the pier entrance but the whole edifice was situated inside the pier; it would be impossible for anyone to leave without coming out either by the pier turnstile or by the Pavilion foyer. Nathaniel, sprinting round to the front and out on to the promenade, stood a little to one side and watched. He hadn't been there half a minute before she emerged, like a late-leaving member of the audience, from the main doors. She was wearing a camel-hair coat and a headscarf knotted below her chin.

It was all going to be difficult, Nathaniel realized. Nobody in their right senses would believe that Big Chief's little assistant had attracted any specific attention for herself. He would have no ready excuse for waylaying her but, acting on impulse, he did so. So excited was he and so unlike his usual self that he actually put a finger under her chin and raised her face to a better light.

'Yes,' he mused thoughtfully.

She was extremely nervous but she was also clearly not unused to casual meetings with men. She was not formally polite but stated at once that he must be a detective sent after her by Ernest Millage. He did not contradict her but allowed her to believe so until he had thought up a better explanation. They walked slowly away from the pier along the almost deserted promenade from circle of light to circle of light cast on the pavement by the tall standards.

Her nervousness subsided. The conversation prospered, an understanding was reached. Ernest must understand, she said, that he didn't need her. It wasn't that she didn't love Ernest, she wouldn't go into that now, but his life was complete without her. After all, she had her life to live; Ernest couldn't expect to keep her cooped up with nothing to do indefinitely. He was selfish, and he was jealous. But how, Nathaniel asked, could he both be complete without her and jealous? No, there was more wrong than that. But, in the meantime, would she come out to supper with him?

Great strength was added to his request by the purely fortuitous fact that they were now passing the Empire Hotel and that the old Rolls was still standing suave and gallant where he had left her.

'I've got my car there,' he said casually.

No, she didn't think she ought to. Doxie Lee would expect to find her in bed when he got back and there would be trouble if she were not. 'That's Big Chief,' she said simply, 'he gets ever so fierce.'

He dismissed Big Chief in a few words of one syllable.

'You don't understand. I'm living with him. His wife's died, her that was Minnehaha. He was desperate three months back. I met him in Obergurgle's, that's the agents; he got himself fixed up with Wulfie Lyon, and he pays me. He was all cut up about his wife and I . . . well,' she said modestly, 'I've been able to cheer him up.'

It was maddening not to be able to see her face properly, the face that had haunted him, and had dwelt with Jason Cragg so that it had driven him to God knew what indiscretions. Notwithstanding her ready admission of adultery, she was as respectable as a church hymnal; shocked at the idea that the man with whom she was living should know she was out with An Other.

'Look,' he said urgently, 'there's Tom's Chop House at Saxon, nine miles up the coast. They're open till all hours. I'm ravenous; I don't know about you but I guess it will do you good to have a steak and chips.'

He had edged her over towards the car and it was that stately automobile that decided her. She'd be tickled pink, she stated, to go out in that. She'd go, she said, if he'd make it snappy.

CHAPTER VI

He had only been able to look away from her lovely face for long enough to feed himself. Now, after several large glasses of Pimm's No. 1, he relaxed over the black coffee and did some curious remembering.

There was Jason's voice remembered: 'Would you say that was the face of a murderess, Ian?'

'There is no typical murderer's face.'

'But a woman could have killed York. I have made certain of that. Does she look what you might call a psychotic personality?'

'What exactly do you mean by a psychotic personality?'

'I don't know, but that's what they say a murderer is if he isn't either a mental defective or a split personality.'

'I think you'll find "psychotic personality" is a very loose term. And people generally show signs of being psychotics before they commit anything so drastic as murder.'

He remembered that.

And he remembered that hand-written memorandum which Jason had showed him. 'York's little wife, bless her, has taken this business marvellously, on top of the murder itself. She's doing her poor best to help me and she's been scraping her memory. Read this – it's a bit thin in places – but I did ask her to do all she could to help and this is the result.'

He remembered reading it through most carefully and, after he had handed it back, Jason had said: 'I don't say anything is exactly untrue, but it's a lot of hooey. There's only one solid fact, only one thing young Easter says she *knows.*'

'That York spent some time with her in Paris?'

'Yes.' Jason was tearing the 'memorandum' into fragments. 'Useless,' he declared.

Nathaniel looked at her thoughtfully. There was a marked diversity in the way she did her hair.

'Do you wear a wig during your act?'

She nodded. 'Big Chief's marvellous, isn't he? He's never looking for work for long. He gives the public something. And it's dangerous! Lots of people think it's a trick, but not it! It's no trick, believe me.'

She leaned forward earnestly. 'There's real petrol in that bowl he dips the torch into. The cotton in the top of the torch soaks it up. It scared me silly the first time I saw it, I can tell you. But he's been doing it all his life and his father did it before him. He's a real, genuine, honest-to-goodness fire-eater. He's modest about it, too; he says it's all a matter of the angle you hold the torch at and the way you breathe. He deliberately breathes petrol fumes in and sets light to the puffs as he jerks them out. He's upset inside sometimes, gets frightful indigestion and it makes him irritable. And he has burns round his mouth now and again.'

She stabbed out her cigarette thoughtfully. 'You see, he really needs someone to look after him, and even though he gets in a paddy and gets a bit rough, too, at times, I'm fond of him.'

'Are you Irish?'

'No.' She looked directly at him with her wide-open eyes. 'Are you?'

'No. I just wondered. Have you ever been to Paris?'

'Yes, often. Look, duck, I've had a lovely time but I must be getting back. He's gone off with the comedians to the billiards hall and I don't think he'll be back before midnight, but I must get back first. And it's rather late at night to begin a discussion about Ernest, don't you think?'

In the car on the way back she remarked thoughtfully:

'Ernest must be using the money he's put on one side for a car. To think he's throwing away money like that, all over getting me back. I mean to say, it don't cost him nothing to get a posh guy like you.'

At the present moment she seemed bitterly disappointing, Nathaniel thought, as he must have known she would be. Psychotic personality? Maybe, but he didn't think so, somehow.

It was Doxie Lee the fire-eater he wanted to meet now, because if Doxie hadn't got much else, he had a Motive.

Fantastic character though the fire-eater appeared to be, he fitted into the motive all right. There was now a complete set of circumstances: York and his actress-mistress, then York marrying and the mistress-habit not quite leaving him; Valentine Millage, trying to make a successful marriage, yet yearning after her past state; Valentine leaving her husband and returning to the stage where she becomes the mistress of the recently widowed music-hall performer; York jealous; the fire-eater jealous of York; jealousy the basis of three-quarters of the premeditated murders. QED.

Fictional? Yes. But Nathaniel returned to his theme-song, that ran like nerve-fibre through all his reckonings: murder must have a plan, a blue-print. The blue-print had to be planned and, if it were planned and the murder did not take place, it was fiction; if the murder did take place, then it was no longer fiction but plain bitter fact.

That, then, could be the blue-print for York's murder.

Jason's murder followed because Jason was too inquisitive and too successful in his enquiries.

Under the heading of jealousy, suspicion lay equally heavily upon Millage. And opportunity, possibly, even more heavily.

And now, driving along the main road to Liverton-upon-Sands from Saxon under the livid sodium lighting, Nathaniel glanced sideways at his companion. She was nodding, on the verge of sleep. Her face appeared a ghastly colour, her lips black, she looked like the plate of her own photograph.

But she knew Nathaniel was looking at her. 'You're very quiet,' she murmured.

Inwardly he cursed. If he could have produced the photograph now and challenged her with it, how simplified the situation would be. She would know instantly that he knew – well, almost everything. No doubt Easter had acted from the best of motives, poor kid; a kind of desperate loyalty to her dead husband had blinded her to the overwhelming advantage that possession of the photograph gave them. With the photograph as a fulcrum, he could lever a confession out of someone. Without it, he had to creep about on the thinnest of ice. One thing, however, was quite certain; he must get to know Valentine and the fire-eater a great deal better and with this end in view he turned the car up a side-turning and came to a stop amongst the sandhills with the tufts of sharp grass sprouting here and there.

She turned towards him automatically and wound herself round him like an affectionate spring. He kissed her passionately, loving her directness and loving, too, her warm, soft lips. It was very, very nice and he went on for a long time.

'It's all wrong,' he said at last, 'to say that a happily married man with an affectionate, beautiful wife, cannot enjoy making love to someone else. In fact,' he enlarged, 'if you stop to think it out, it's a compliment to the aforesaid wife.'

'Well I never!' she chuckled. 'That's a new one on me!'

He kissed her until he exclaimed: 'God, I'm seeing stars!'

'Yes.' She wriggled herself off his knee and back into her seat. 'We'd best be getting along.'

More than slightly intoxicated, he pursued a dog-eared theme: 'Why don't you go back to your husband? Why do you racket about with this gipsy-guy? You know how you'll end up if you go on like this, don't you?'

'Why should I tell you?' she asked primly.

'After all that kissing, I think you might,' Nathaniel observed, aggrieved.

She chuckled, then said: 'Marriage is one thing and making love's another. It don't surprise me at all that Ernest's got one of these private detectives . . .'

'Meaning me?'

'Meaning you. It don't surprise me at all. But that don't mean I've got to talk to you about my marriage. That's my business.'

He was beginning to like her very much. 'You're right,' he said thoughtfully. 'Nothing is more personal, yet nothing excites other people's interest quite so much. Only the protagonists know what goes on behind its smooth face.'

She was applying lipstick by the light from the dashboard. 'What's that, when it's at home?'

Nathaniel laughed lightly as he backed the car. 'I must meet your human candelabra.'

'You'd better not! He's got a temper, I can tell you. He's told me more than once he'd give me a black eye if I carried on with anyone else and there's one of the comedians in the show . . . Well, never mind that.'

They were back on the main road now. 'If you ask me,' Nathaniel observed, 'that's just what you need. If Ernest Millage had given you a few black eyes we wouldn't be where we are now.'

And York: where did he come in?

'Ernest has never laid a finger on me in anger,' she said soberly.

'More fool he. Now, where am I to take you?'

'We've rooms in Southsea Road, off the prom. But you'd best drop me at the pier. I'll tell him I've been with some of the other girls, if he's back before me.'

Liverton-upon-Sands had gone to bed; it lay like a sleeping turtle under its greenish lights. The clock on the plain face of the Baptist church showed it to be a few minutes to midnight. A turning off the main road led straight down to the promenade, the pier and the sea, and it was as they were gliding silently between the closed shop fronts of this street that they passed a gaggle of men, straggling down the streets in ones and twos, shouting and laughing. At the red lights of a crossing they were obliged to stop and the group of men caught up with the car.

Though Big Chief was now wearing a cloth cap and a turtle-necked sweater, Nathaniel recognized him from his hawk-like profile from which the remains of kohl markings and greasepaint had been but poorly removed. He thrust his fierce face against the window with such suddenness that Nathaniel felt he had been hit by a tomahawk.

'Now then, now then!'

Valentine fumbled with the window handle, whilst he stood with his face terrifyingly close and made noises like a growling dog. She got it lowered at last. 'This gentleman took us out to supper at Saxon,' she said breathlessly, 'me and two others. We've dropped the others and he's just taking me back.'

Why tell a lie that could be so easily proved? Nat leaned over her and drew back the door catch. 'Care for a lift?'

The traffic lights had turned from green to red again. 'Thanks.' Yet undeflated he stepped inside with some dignity. The front seat was so wide that it was scarcely necessary to move closer to Nat, but she did. They glided past Big Chief's erstwhile companions, who all looked tactfully ahead, and in a ghastly silence they reached the pier. Out of the side of his mouth, Big Chief dropped instructions and presently they drew up at the lodgings.

'Go on in,' he ordered, jerking his thumb at Valentine. In his present state of mind, Nat felt it wiser to say nothing. He nodded briskly at the two of them, his foot on the clutch ready to depart.

But Valentine was not one to forget her manners. 'Thank

you for the pleasant evening.' She leaned across in front of the gipsy and gave her hand formally. She also gave Nat a slow, delightful wink.

'Cut along,' the fire-eater barked impatiently, and then he put his extraordinary face inside the car rather unpleasantly close to Nat's own face. He smelled strongly of stale beer but so did Nat.

'If you've got'ny sense, you'll keep off. Get me?'

'I get you.' Nat smiled, managing with some difficulty not to laugh. The look Big Chief gave him and the sound he made were remarkably like that of Captain Hook in *Peter Pan* when he creeps in and shakes his hook at the audience with a fantastic leer and a 'Grr ... rr' that sends shivers of apprehension down the spine.

CHAPTER VII

'I'll swear,' the fire-eater boasted, amid general laughter, 'that I've never struck a woman with anything bigger than half a brick.' Though he could not be said to expand exactly, under the influence of an admiring audience, he certainly intensified, became more so, as it were.

In Nat's experience there was almost no situation which could not be clarified by the liberal application of alcohol; he made it his business the following day to get as much drink as possible inside Big Chief in the short time available. And now he had the pleasure of sitting quietly in the background, watching the result of his expenditure.

As a fire-eater it was the fire that impressed rather than the man; without his flaming petrol torches, he was as ineffectual as a gas-cooker without the gas. But off the stage, now that one saw him in the round, the man made an impact. There was something of the mystic about him, something of the brooding, introverted 'outsider'. His dark hair and skin, his curiously high voice and strange intonation, the high cheekbones and beetling frown made him something of a phenomenon. There was a refinement about him deriving from his Hindu blood and Yoga-practising progenitors, upon which his present boastful, pub-crawling manner lay incongruously.

'So she's been warned. She knows where she gets off. One woman at a time, that's my motto.' Loud laughter and a burst of lubricous wit greeted this sally.

There's a rake-hell for you, Nat thought, but did he stab first York and then Jason because he was jealous of the woman of the moment? Prematurely aged (he was twenty-nine and looked fifty), there was a faint air of desperation about him. Undoubtedly the hazards of his occupation pre-destined him for an early death; did these same hazards also affect his mind? The lining of his stomach must be in a ghastly state, Nat thought, and the lines on his face were caused, no doubt, by constant pain.

If the fire-eater had been an ordinary person, guilt could have been proved, or disproved, by the process of going backwards through time, week after week, to the two relevant dates. Where was he when first York was murdered, and then Jason?

Nat had gone into this with him as far as it was possible without causing annoyance and it appeared that shortly after the day in the autumn when he had met Valentine Millage at the agents, they had been touring the North of England. And that was as far as it would go.

The fire-eater and Minnehaha travelled in a not very plain van, rather reminiscent of a henhouse on wheels, known affectionately in the profession as 'the privy'. It had a good old Austin engine in front of the amateurishly-built body and was painted a bright yellow. 'Big Chief' was splashed in large red lettering across the yellow, 'and Minnehaha' appeared below in much smaller letters of a sober black, on either side of the van. It was an almost farcical thought that anyone should set off on a murder-trip in such a vehicle.

Both the Craggs had been murdered on a weekday; could the gipsy have made an involved journey from the North of England to London and thence to Putney by trains and Underground without being absent from his work longer than twenty-four hours? Yes, he could, and with time to spare.

But *would* he?

That was something which Nat intended to find out.

Unfortunately, the clarity of his mind was clouded by the insane desire to see Valentine alone. It was madness to allow personal feelings to enter into an investigation of this kind, but there it was . . .

Nat considered his vulnerability to women a handicap; it was more than time he grew out of it, but at the same time he made no great effort to overcome it. I'm nearly middle-aged, he used to think, and then it will be all over. But now he really was middle-aged, and it wasn't over, not nearly.

Though he had been with the gipsy all day he had not been able to see Valentine other than on the stage at the evening performance in her ridiculous disguise of Minne-haha, and he was now planning to get Big Chief so drunk that he could slip away from the Dun Cow and see her for a few moments, at least, at her lodgings in Southsea Road.

The gipsy was drunk now, but only up to a point, and it was already closing-time.

'The privy' and the Rolls were parked side by side on a piece of spare ground at the side of the public house; neither of them being in the least class-conscious, they waited with dignity for their owners who presently approached a trifle uncertainly. Big Chief suggested, with a bellow of laughter, that they exchange vehicles. Nathaniel looked at him closely. If he had been to the house in Putney on that cold January night that Jason Cragg was murdered, Big Chief could not have failed to see the old car parked in the drive, immediately outside the house. If he had, then he must know that Nathaniel's meeting with him was not a chance one. If he had murdered Jason for knowing too much, then he would now murder Nat, and probably using the same successful method as before. What was going on behind those hooded eyes, that insolent, drunken expression?

It being closing time, a dozen or so drinkers from the bar had followed them out and now stood about in a shouting, laughing group after the manner of men at closing time.

Nathaniel, proud of his car, was perfectly determined not to let Big Chief, or anyone else, drive it, but he was also anxious to continue in the role of jolly-good-fellow that he had spent the day in building up so carefully. He laughed good-naturedly, murmuring that he was sure the 'privy' could knock spots off the Rolls for speed.

At once a marathon was planned and someone offered to make a book. 'Two to one, bar one' and tick-tack movements confused the situation. Fierce argument as to the relative accomplishments of each vehicle broke out.

With the watchful bobby no longer on the beat, minor rioting broke out. The two vehicles were pushed out on to the now empty High Street and there was a general scramble for seats. It was now quite an impossibility to retain his popularity and not agree to the race.

'But no passengers,' Nathaniel said firmly. 'If I crash there's only me,' he shouted. 'I don't want to have to keep any of your families for the rest of my life.' This seemed reasonable enough and most people fell back. A fat man appointed himself official starter and the route was described to Nat. They were to race along the promenade as far as the amusement park, up the sandy track on to the main road and back along the main road and down the High Street to the Dun Cow. Roughly two miles. The fat man took out his stopwatch.

There was a great deal of fooling and bets were actually made. Big Chief cleared everyone out of his van and, hitching up his trousers with a gesture of determination, he climbed in and grimly started up his engine. A coin was tossed for position on the road and the Rolls was brought level with the van.

It's madness, Nat thought, but he had no intention of racing. He would let Big Chief career ahead, so far ahead that there would be no need for him to drive recklessly, and they would return to the pub unimpaired, having appeared to be a couple of daredevils, no bones broken, honour and sportsmanship intact.

The fat man stood on the edge of the kerb with a handkerchief held ludicrously, limply from its extreme corner. 'Have you got your engine running, mister?' he asked Nat incredulously. 'Can't hear a bloomin' thing!'

No one could fail to hear the engine of the 'privy' which Big Chief was revving-up importantly. 'Are you ready now, gennelmen?' the fat man asked. 'OFF!'

It was a false start; shouts of laughter and warning cries stopped them. One humorist had climbed into the boot and pulled the lid down on top of himself; when the Rolls started he had been unable to keep the joke to himself, had raised the lid and waved farewell to the watching crowd. He was pulled out and the lid thumped back into place; Nathaniel cursed himself for not locking it.

'There is no one else in there, is there?' he asked with comic good-humour.

On being assured that there was not, he signalled to the fat man, who again got himself into position with the handkerchief.

'One,' he puffed, 'two, three and OFF!'

With an impressive roar from its Brooklands silencer the 'privy' was off, rocking and rolling down the High Street towards the pier and round the left-hand corner on to the promenade at a terrifying angle, on two of its wooden-spoked wheels. Nathaniel caught him up on the straight, but a glance at the grim face at the driving wheel told him that the gipsy was in dead earnest.

All right, Nat thought with a stab of excitement, and pressed the accelerator down. Fifty, sixty, sixty-five, seventy . . . the 'privy' was still ahead, but so was the fun fair, shuttered and closed down now, but undoubtedly there. Nat slowed down, ready for the second left-hand turn on to the cinder track.

He yelled: 'Slow down, you fool!' and pressed the horn continuously in warning, but incredibly the 'privy' went forging on with the inexorability of a satellite, ploughing its way through the wooden fence; staying miraculously upright, it bumped its way right into the heart of the group of light wooden kiosks with all the abandon of an old Ford in a custard-pie comedy film in the early days. It came to a standstill only because at last it toppled over sideways. It was not more than twenty yards into the fun fair but that twenty yards was now a very depressed area indeed.

As Nat picked his way over the debris, Big Chief, the Human Candelabra, emerged from the upward door of the van like a wounded and furious wasp.

'Are you hurt?' Nat cried.

'No,' was the answer, 'but you're going to be!' As the angry man advanced upon him, Nat had a grateful thought for the Japanese he met in Burma who had taught him the two useful ju-jutsu throws he knew.

'It was a trick,' Big Chief shouted, 'a big bloody, mean trick! And it came off, yes, it came off . . . but you'll pay for it.' He was standing only a couple of yards away now and his anger was as tangible as the flames which at other times he blasted from his mouth. Involuntarily Nat stepped back.

'I'll bash you to pulp,' Big Chief shouted drunkenly, 'and I don't care if I swing for it, you bleedin' little swindlin' toff. I know your sort; take a fancy to another man's girl and you've got to have her. You inherit the world, eh? Take that, you stuffed swank, and that, you rotten little pimp.'

Though he had had time to prepare, Nat was not ready for a fight, he wasn't feeling like fighting, he seldom did. He was suffering from drink and shock and a certain lassitude. The first blow woke him up, the second hurt very much indeed and the pain roused him to violent anger. Stepping back for momentum, he darted forward, butted his head into Big Chief's crutch and took hold of his legs in the way he had been taught. Up went Big Chief, as though he had been tossed in a blanket, up and over Nat's head and through the air like an autumn leaf; he landed, grunting with pain, on the corner of the overturned fortune-teller's tent. A wealth of fascinating appellations flowed from his lips but Nat did not stay to listen.

CHAPTER VIII

Now, Nat realized as he drove slowly back along the promenade, past the Empire Hotel, was the time for the evening to be brought to a close. He ought to go into his hotel, go to bed and leave things to sort themselves out. But he seldom chose the path of discretion.

The return to the Dun Cow was a shocking anti-climax.

The race, which only a few minutes before had seemed amusing, a subject for laughter and re-telling with more laughter, now appeared the most childish and puerile of pranks. For a man of Nat's standing (and, indeed, age) it was unbelievably silly. It just goes to show, Nat thought in a highly unsatisfactory extenuation, how alcohol cripples judgement.

Everyone was looking up the High Street for the first appearance of the victor. Nat drew up almost silently behind the riotous crowd before he was noticed. 'I don't know what happened,' he told everyone. 'He went crashing on into the middle of the fun fair instead of turning off up the cinder track. It was poorly lighted. I don't think he's badly hurt.'

It was a little difficult to state satisfactorily why he had not brought Big Chief back with him. 'He's fighting mad,' he tried to explain. 'Somebody had better take a doctor along, he's concussed, perhaps. Couldn't keep his hands off me.' He was determined not to return to the fun fair. 'Look, I'll go and find a doctor, and if somebody could telephone for an ambulance . . . he'd better be taken to hospital for a check-up. The van's wrecked.'

One or two of them had cars and motor-cycle combinations of their own; the accident had a sobering effect; they quickly organized themselves into a helpful unit. Some of them went off to the hospital to collect an ambulance, and the rest, anxious not to miss anything, set off for the scene of the accident.

Nobody had mentioned the woman and she must certainly be told. Nat had spent most of the day in Big Chief's company. The only opportunity the gipsy could have had of finding out exactly which girls were *not* with Nat and his Valentine the previous evening was during the evening performance at the Pavilion. Why, then, had he not at once challenged Nat? Why had he agreed to come to drink at the Dun Cow after the show and appeared reasonably friendly? Whatever the reason, it told Nat that Big Chief had more than his share of low cunning. Perhaps he had planned to murder Nat, to stab him in the back that evening, given a suitable opportunity.

The more he thought of it the more convincing it seemed. They would all have said good night and dispersed, Big Chief climbing into his van and leaving with the rest. Then Big Chief leaving his van, possibly outside the pier, where it so often stood, and going swiftly to the Empire Hotel, waylaying Nat as he closed up his car for the night, strolling with him along the promenade, a pretext for talking things over and then, up some quiet turning, the stabbing . . . that skilful, deadly successful stabbing. Perhaps the stupid race had saved Nat's life.

There would have been no suspicions directed at Big Chief, for had they not been seen together all day, in and out of the public houses of Liverton-upon-Sands, and again after the evening performance, the best of friends?

Nat felt his palms wet with sweat on the steering wheel.

All this seemed very far from being mere fancy when he met Valentine in the dark, narrow little hall of her stuffy lodging house. He told her, quickly, everything that had happened.

'I knew it,' she declared, 'I knew something was going to happen! He found out from the girls that no one had been to Saxon with us last night. I could tell, when we was doing the act . . . he was shaking with rage and he snatched the torches off me. He would have beaten you up and then come back and beaten me up!' She said it almost proudly.

Nat gazed at her incredulously. 'How can you stand it?'

'It makes a change after Ernest,' she said. 'I could shake Ernest, he is that tame.' Nat took heart from the use of the present tense.

'I'd leave the bruiser,' he advised urgently. 'He's had a good shaking up, I'm sure they'll keep him in hospital a day or so, you won't have the act tomorrow.'

She clicked her tongue: 'Tt – tt! And it's matinee day, too, Saturday!'

She's so superficial, Nat thought, that she's mentally unapproachable, she doesn't seem to feel. It is only when you have her in your arms that she's anything at all and, to add verisimilitude to his thesis, he did that, winding her round him, in the narrow, dark hall, and kissing her passionately.

She's not a tart, he thought, exactly, but she's a splendid vehicle for kissing et cetera, and laughed at his own ambiguity, focalized in the et cetera.

'Look,' he said, setting her upright. 'You'll never do any good with this man, and you know it, at the bottom of your heart. You're just a good-time gal, and you aren't getting any younger. Why not drop it before you get badly hurt? You'll end up as a frowsty old tart and then you won't even be that, you'll be a bent, crippled, lined old woman creeping out into the Edgware Road, clutching your shabby purse with the remains of your weekly old-age allowance in it, off to buy yourself half a pint of milk . . . or bitter.'

He was holding her gently now, whispering into the pixie ear which he could not see but knew to be there.

'You've got a good man there in London who adores you and wants you back. Why not go back to him and settle down and have children to love and to look after you in your old age? Youth doesn't last for ever, you know.' He pulled the ear gently. 'You haven't all the time in the world left to have children. They're worth having, believe me . . .'

Nat put everything he had into his plea. Though he had no proof against the fire-eater as yet, he had resolved to put his suspicions before the CID and if Big Chief were ever to be arrested, it was going to be extremely unpleasant for his female assistant. Nat did not give a damn about Ernest Millage but he was certainly the answer to his lawful wife's present predicament.

'You're so lucky,' Nat hissed, 'to have that man devoted to you, ready to forgive, because when all's said and done, you have let him down, done the dirty . . .'

Somewhere upstairs in the smelly little house a thin door banged; somebody had clearly been doing their best to overhear, and that same person had possibly gone back into their room to look out of the window and examine the Rolls by the light of the nearby lamp-post.

'Come now,' Nat pressed her. 'Drive back to London with me now. It will save a lot of trouble.'

'He'd be after us, don't you worry!'

'What in? The van's smashed up!'

'No . . .' Valentine said uncertainly.

'Don't tell me you love him! Just don't tell me that because I'll never believe it.'

'No, I don't exactly love him but I don't want to go back and live my old life in Edgware. Rosedale . . .'

'You can't do that,' Nat said wildly, carried away by his own verbosity, 'you'll not do that; it's let to a West African woman with a lot of black kids,' and then cursed himself inwardly for his indiscretion.

'How do you know?' she asked, turning her great eyes round to his own alarmed ones. 'Well, that settles it! If Ernest has gone back to his mother that settles it!' And, tearing herself from Nat's arms, she ran upstairs.

But he knew she was crying and he was not without hope as he let himself out quietly.

CHAPTER IX

'Sam,' Mrs Bacon addressed as much of her husband as she could see beneath the extended evening paper, his uniform trousers and his feet in thick grey socks. A tray holding cups of cocoa and a plate of sandwiches between them, they were watching the television, Sam reading his newspaper and Mrs Bacon darning a clean pair of Sam's grey socks.

'Yes, love?'

'About those Cragg murders . . .'

'Coo, what a morbid mind!'

'Well, somebody's going to win that Five Thousand.'

'Not necessary-ly.'

'I bin thinkin'.'

'Don't do it,' Sam advised. 'It's only nuts and crackpots that gets thinking. You should see some of the folk who've bin thinking about that money . . . cranky, nothink less! It's giving us some work, I can tell you. The ole man says: "You never know," he says, "the one you think is the biggest dud of the lot may turn out to be the one that's got the answer." Dozens of people have turned up with bits of damn silly information. But you mark my words, it's nobody in this country done it; it's an international crook, like I've said all along, cooling his heels in the Kremlin now, shouldn't wonder.'

Mrs Bacon looked crushed but still puzzled. 'What, exactly, does it mean by *information leading to the arrest*?'

'Just what it says. The trouble is that folk bring you along information that leads nowhere.'

'Would a vital clue be *information leading to the arrest*?'

Sam Bacon lowered his paper and looked with interest at his wife, exhaling breath through his front teeth as he did so. 'Vital clue!' He gave a great belly laugh. 'You and your *vital clues*. Doris, the Richmond sleuth, eh?'

But Doris did not join in the laughter. 'Who would you take your vital clue to?' she asked.

'My old man, of course.' Sam's laughter over, he returned to the newspaper, but was overtaken by a further attack of wit. 'If I see you coming, I'll say to the inspector, I'll say: "Here comes my old woman with a vital clue!"' He became convulsed. 'He'll get me to go out and tell you what you can do with it!'

Mrs Sam looked thoughtfully at her husband over the top of her glasses. She was not amused.

CHAPTER X

He awoke at eight with less of a hangover than he deserved. There was a painful area in the vicinity of his gallbladder and he had a stiff neck, but he was able to eat a good breakfast and about ten o'clock he strolled out of the dining-room with the daily paper under his arm.

She was just paying off a taxi and the doorman was carrying in a variety of gaudy and unsuitable luggage. Nat stared in some horror at the galaxy of zip-fasteners, plaid material and imitation light-weight pigskin, but more in terror of what they represented than their actual appearance.

'Yes,' she stated unnecessarily, as the doorman withdrew some yards with a discreet cough, 'I've come. I haven't slept a wink all night, thinking over what you said. So here I am.'

'That's fine!' Nat smiled brightly, acting as ever, on impulse. He examined closely her charming, upturned face, full of trust. It is always difficult to read accurately the thoughts of a woman who gives her body generously but has nothing else to offer. Did she mean she had decided to return to Ernest or . . . ?

'Where can we talk?' she asked, looking round.

'Out in the car is the safer place.'

'Shall I bring out the luggage?' the doorman asked officiously.

Yes, of course. Nat raised the lid of the boot whilst the porter piled the luggage into its vast interior. Of course, it was the only way.

'Listen –' she grasped his arm with warm strong fingers, when they were inside the car – 'the police have been round this morning. Doxie wasn't injured, like you said. He's been discharged from hospital this morning and he's round at the police station now. They came to tell me. There's going to be a lot of trouble about last night's affair; over the insurance, see? Doxie's making all kinds of wild statements about you and the police'll be coming round here to get your side of the story.'

'That's all right. Everything is perfectly straightforward as far as I'm concerned.'

'I guess so, but you was an eye-witness of the accident; the insurance people will want your story too.'

'Is that all?'

'Look,' she said nervously. 'Don't waste time. Let's beat it. Doxie's going to half kill you if he sees you. He says he'll give you the biggest thrashing of your life, that you planned the race and all the rest of it. He's reckless, that one, he doesn't give a fig for going to gaol for a few weeks for assault; it gives his insides a bit of a rest from fire-eating. He always comes out feeling better. It'll hurt if he gets at you, believe you me!'

'I'm sure it will,' Nat said, uneasily feeling his sore ribs.

'It's this bloomin' great car,' she complained, 'so conspicuous, be seen all over the place.'

Nat thought. He thought about the new modern house in Putney in its garden of rhododendrons. He saw Easter sitting by the log fire in her charming sitting-room; pale and withdrawn and lonely, awaiting his return. Waiting ... perhaps reading one of her innumerable rag mags to pass away the time, perhaps idly turning on the radiogram; listening for the door bell, listening for the telephone and jumping nervously at the sound of either. Easter.

He saw the outline of a diabolical plan. A plan of which the details must be filled in by circumstance, but nonetheless ... devilish.

'Just one sec,' he said. 'I'll get my bag and pay my bill and I'll be with you.'

'All right, dear,' she agreed cheerfully, following him back to the hotel, 'but give me time to brighten myself up in the "Ladies".'

CHAPTER XI

After paying his bill, Nat handed the receptionist a slip of paper on which he had written: N. Sapperton, 2 Silverdale, Putney, S.W.

'Look,' he said, 'the police will be here today about that accident along at the fun fair last night; I was an eye-witness. But I've got to rush back to London and they'll have to get in touch with me there. Give them this address, will you? Now don't lose it; if they try to get hold of me through the registration number of my car they'll find it's in another name and address. But don't panic, there's a good girl. Everything's okey dokey!' Wishing very much that it were, Nat gave her one of his most charming smiles and departed.

With deep interest Nat watched Valentine Millage step into the car whilst the doorman held the door open for her; she settled herself with the ease of a regular Rolls traveller, giving the doorman a curt nod. His face was a study.

So that, Nat thought, as they slid away from the Empire Hotel, and from Liverton-upon-Sands, is how she slips out of the lives of her lovers, without a backward look. *Le roi est mort, vive le roi* . . .

Ernest Millage, Doxie Lee . . . and York Cragg? Did she leave York or did he leave her? Seen in the whole, Valentine was an unlikely mistress for York; for one thing, she did not dress well and York had been fussy about women's clothes. In the arms, however, she was better than most, and possibly York never saw her dressed. That, in crude fact, was the only way in which Nat could see York in love with Valentine, and he sympathized. How secret was York's secret life and how bitterly unfair it was that it had to be exposed in all its cheapness. And yet, if a man knew that his most foolish peccadillo would be laid open to universal judgement after his death, would it make him any more careful? Was it, perhaps, worth it?

'You're very quiet, dear,' Valentine observed. 'Thinking? A penny for them.'

'I'm thinking about York Cragg.' Perhaps it was unwise to mention his name when he was driving and therefore unable to observe the result.

'Who's he, when he's at home?'

The edges of Nat's teeth felt as uncomfortable as though someone had scraped the blade of a knife against china.

'He was the son of a very old friend. He's dead.'

'Tt . . . tt . . . tt.'

Nat drew to the side of the road and stopped the car rather hurriedly. He turned to Valentine, looking at her directly and with a serious face.

'York Cragg,' he said clearly and slowly, 'the son of Sir Jason Cragg, the shipping magnate.' Had she, in fact, gone slightly red? She had certainly not paled. Perhaps it was his own behaviour which was embarrassing her.

Nat re-started the car. She was by way of being an actress, he must remember. He also reminded himself that she could not have known York under an assumed name; he could see now the actressy scribble at the bottom of her photograph: 'To my darling York . . .'

'You are acting queer,' she remarked. 'What's up? Getting cold feet, are you? Worrying about the wife and kiddies?'

'No. They are the last thing I am worrying about. My wife is in Sweden for two months' holiday with her parents. The children are with her. And, by the way, I love my wife.'

'Why aren't you with her, then?'

'Business,' he said shortly.

'Oh, you businessmen! You beat me!'

'We don't, that's the trouble!'

She giggled. 'Where are we off to now?'

'To London. It is Saturday, by the way. Haven't you let down Doxie Lee's act rather badly?'

'He'll get someone to do my job, never fear. I've left the clothes and the wig and all at the Pavilion; he'll get one of the other girls for today's performances, anyway.'

'What would have happened if he'd been badly hurt last night? What would Mr Wulfie Lyon have had to say?'

She shrugged. 'There's a notice in the programme that the management aren't responsible for anyone failing to go on.'

'I always thought "the show must go on" was the most important thing in an actor's life.'

'Well, dear, it's not quite the same in this sort of show.'

'I see. Then Doxie Lee, the Human Candelabra, can simply walk out, can he?'

'It's not as easy as that. We're playing Huddersfield next week; Doxie'll have to get himself fixed up with someone before Monday.'

'You know damn well he won't! He'll be after you, Valentine.'

'What would be the use? He doesn't even know your name. And I've got no address at the moment, so how can he find me? Besides, the van's smashed up.'

'There are always trains to London.'

She was quiet for a long time and then she said: 'He'd kill me, you know. Not that he loves me all that much, it's just his temper-ment. He's a real gipsy and gipsy women are faithful; he gave me a long jaw about that when he took me on. I was as good as a wife, he said. It was after I'd left Ernest and was on the road with Doxie he came up with all that. Quite shook up, I was.'

'You don't give yourself time to think, do you? Well, I sympathize, I'm rather like that myself.'

'It was a bit of a school kid he had helping him after his wife died. There was nothing whatever between them; she was one of these stage-struck kids. He sent her home to her mum when he caught up with me.' She was quiet again for some time. 'Yes,' she went on gloomily, 'gipsies are, what do you call it, mono . . . mono what's its.'

'Monogamists. Married to only one at a time.'

She nodded. 'That's right. Regular old-fashioned. I took no notice,' she said comfortably. 'I thought, when I've had enough of Doxie, I thought, that'll be it.'

I bet you did, Nat agreed.

'Well, the world's a big place, he'll have a job finding me, unless he traces us through your car number! This bloomin' car!'

'You could hardly be more conspicuous if you had ridden off on a white charger.'

After which sobering thought they drove for many miles in silence.

Nat was pleased that he was able to pick out his own patient way, down, as he called it, through the rural heart of England, after his years abroad. They stopped for lunch at an excellent hotel at Bakewell in Derbyshire.

Though he had no cocktails himself he gave her two martinis before the wine which they had with lunch, and when he had got her in what he considered to be the right state of mind he said: 'I expect you'll be very surprised to hear that I'm going to put you into an hotel tonight. Don't worry, I'll pay the bill but I won't be there myself. There are certain things to be attended to. It isn't that I don't want to sleep with you but you'll be surprised to hear that there are more pressing things I have to do.'

'I'm not fussy.'

No, you're not, he thought. Very far from it.

'I trust you absolutely!'

You would!

'I know a gentleman when I see one.'

'I'm not impressed with your judgement, all the same. Your husband is a good little chap; you made a big mistake walking out on him.'

Her face took on a curiously puffy, almost stupid look.

'Come on, out with it. You may as well tell me the lot!'

'I don't know how much you know Ernest. Look,' she said, suddenly and somewhat retardedly anxious. 'If Ernest sent you up to Liverton to get me to go back to him, this wouldn't be quite the way he'd think of your doing it, would it?'

'It was entirely your own idea that Ernest sent me. At least you thought Ernest cared for you enough to do something of the kind. You live for the moment, don't you, Val? What went before, what comes after . . . you couldn't care less . . . could you?' He put his hand affectionately over hers. 'But seriously, Ernest has a case. He took you on as he found you, and I bet that wasn't exactly as a virgin, was it? I mean, to put it mildly. He took you on, for better, for worse. And then, because life isn't madly exciting, you pack your bags and walk out. I'm sorry for Ernest. I'm on his side, if you want to know.'

'Poor Ernest,' she mused, 'and he puts his savings into tracing me. Shows he's keen. Oh, it's such a mix-up.'

'You may as well spill it all to your old uncle. I'm sure to find out sooner or later, so you may as well tell me now.'

Silence. Such beautiful eyes, he thought; with so little behind them, how is it they have any expression at all? Or had they? Was it not simply the way they were made up?

'What was it about Ernest? Is he a pervert, or what?'

'A what?' she gobbled innocently. 'No, dear. It was his mum.'

And so the trite little story came out, the perfect example

of the letter asking the advice of 'Uncle Nat' in *Women Only*: how to deal with the over-possessive mother-in-law.

As she became more and more emotional, Nat looked nervously round at his fellow lunchers, most of whom were now on the point of departure. 'She hates me; for all her smarmy welcome, she meant to get me away from Ernest right from the start. And she's not one you can have a real set-to with; she thinks herself a bit upper-class and she's sarcastic and mean . . . Oh, she's mean! Every evening, on his way home from work, Ernest went in to see her and then home to me with the things that woman had said to him against me written all over his face!'

She wept.

What a very, very rum thing, Nat thought, if she didn't care so very much about Ernest, she cared passionately about her marriage.

'Well, strike a light!' he exclaimed flippantly, but he was moved.

CHAPTER XII

Easter went on living her life: she made a fourth at bridge after dining with the Ramsgates; she lunched the following day with Jill at Scheherazade; she went to a movie in the afternoon; she had her hair done and a manicure at her hairdresser in Dover Street; she went to an art exhibition in Bruton Street. On the Saturday morning she shopped in her car, in Putney High Street. It was dull buying week-end food for one; she bought a small roasting fowl, fruit, bread, a walnut cake. She bought an armful of the newest glossy magazines. She ordered sherry and some half bottles of white wine. She drove back home. She cleaned the car; she dug in the garden; she toasted herself crumpets for tea; she listened to Elvis Presley on the gramophone; she telephoned to Jill; she did a little ironing on the kitchen table.

She made up the sitting-room fire and lay on the sofa reading her magazines; she slept a little; she got up to prepare her supper. She brought her supper into the living-room and ate it upon the low table by the fire. She sat for a long time, thinking. She cleared away and washed up the supper things. She returned to the sitting-room and, turning on the gramophone again, she danced a little, by herself. She turned on the radio and lay on the sofa, one foot swinging, listening to the Saturday-night programme. She went upstairs to her bedroom, drew the curtains, turned on the electric fire, changed into a dressing-gown and came downstairs again. She went into the kitchen to make herself a hot drink. As she stood at the sink, mixing the Horlicks, she moved aside the curtain, out of sheer habit, and looked up at the window in the block of flats.

There was a light!

The shock of seeing the window lighted again, at last, after looking so many times, caused her almost to drop the cup and spoon. She looked at the clock – eleven!

She made her hot drink and returned to the living-room where, suddenly, the telephone had taken on a presence; impersonal, it was very much there, black and crouching and full of foreboding. As she sipped her hot drink she stared at it over the rim of her cup.

Everything that she may have been going to say to Mr Sapperton, né Wainwright, in her earlier fury and bewilderment, had now deserted her. Anger equipped one with ability; in anger one could act constructively, or the reverse. But, at least, one could act. Without it, one could be left wondering miserably what to do, what to say; whether, indeed, to do or to say anything.

Easter clasped her arms round her knees and, sitting on the floor beside the dying fire, she rocked herself slightly to and fro and the telephone leered at her across the hearth in the gentle light from the lamps.

At one o'clock she rose, stiff and chilly, and returned to the kitchen. The light was out in the bedroom. So, for the moment, the question was shelved, there was nothing she need do. Easter crept thankfully to bed.

CHAPTER XIII

Sunday morning has a special character of its own; Easter lay in bed and enjoyed it. York was always fearfully active on a Sunday morning; he would disappear into the boiler room and spend much time working out oil consumption and testing the thermostat; he would potter about with a spanner, tightening things up; he would oil hinges and stop dripping taps. Before lunch they would have friends in for tumblers of Black Velvet and in the early evening, if they were not going out to other friends, they would drive to the West End to see a movie and have a late supper at a restaurant.

Easter lay luxuriously with her creamy arms behind her head and enjoyed doing nothing. How long would it be before Nat came, she wondered? After the fierce frustration of not being able to see him at once, she felt a comfortable patience; he could take his time.

He came at teatime; Easter's sitting-room was flooded with sunlight and heavy with the scent of hyacinths. 'Darling Easter,' he said, after the conventional greetings. 'Will you ever forgive me? I could not have let you know I was going. You'd never have put up with it, or, I should say, there'd have had to be a lot of explanation which, at that time, I was not prepared to give. May I have a piece of this delicious-looking walnut cake?'

She went for another cup and saucer and Nat sat down; he was tired.

'I'm going to tell you all about it, everything. My God!'

he exclaimed. 'Your good husband let himself in for something over that dame.'

Her face tightened. 'I'll never forgive you if you've been meddling in that affair.'

'Of course you'll forgive me. I may as well tell you that the Craggs were my friends as well as being your husband and father-in-law. They were my good friends. I hate to mention my shock and wretchedness when your own must have been so much greater, but, nevertheless, their deaths were a terrible shock.'

'What was the point in keeping your name secret? What was the idea in getting a flat overlooking this house? To spy on me?'

'It was my method, that's all. I wanted to get to know you. I'd heard a lot about you and I didn't want to crash in as a ready-made friend of yours. As it happens, that flat belongs to a chap in the FO and I heard by the grapevine that he wanted to let it for two years, as he's been posted to Bogotà. A married couple I happen to know have taken it, but they agreed to let me have it for a few weeks whilst they're on holiday in Juan. Simple.'

'But why the assumed name?'

'I see.' Nat was thoughtful. 'The Ramsgates. I knew it was bound to come out, just as the Ramsgates, one day, would certainly walk in here. But as it happens it is not an assumed name. Ian Nathaniel Sapperton Wainwright . . . that's me. Nathaniel after a Lancashire grandfather who left me some shares for it, and Sapperton was my mother's name. Still simple, isn't it?'

'I still don't see the point,' Easter said coldly.

'Don't try to, just accept it. I'm one of whom my mother dotingly said: "Boys will be boys." Madcap Ian, the pickled schoolboy, one of those Englishmen who never grow up, if you like. York and Jason would be amongst the first to appreciate the fun I'm having.'

Easter was giving him some curious looks, almost as

though she suspected him of being not quite sane.

'Only I'm beginning to wonder,' Nat went on, 'whether I know anything about my friend York. His amours are unlikely in the extreme.'

'You're absolutely exasperating,' Easter exclaimed, her voice only just avoiding shrillness.

'It is now that things become far from simple,' Nat said, finishing his tea and replacing the cup and saucer carefully on the tray. 'I have managed to run his Valentine, or Mr Millage's Mrs Millage, to earth. She has, in fact, flung herself upon my breast; in other words, got herself into my hair. She is living, or was until yesterday, with a real live (live is the word, he's probably lousy) gipsy, Doxie Lee, or Big Chief, the Human Candelabra. A crazy-mixed-up gipsy.' Nat paused. 'Or is he? And whether this gipsy did or did not murder first York, out of jealousy, and then Jason, because he Knew Too Much, is a simple question of dates. *Where* he was and *when*. And it's so easy – the police are busy on that now – it's so easy to find out where a Human Candelabra is, and when; specially when he goes about in a fearfully conspicuous yellow-painted van with his name in large letters on the side. By tonight the police will know just where he was billed on the night York was killed, and ditto Jason. If he was playing at Brixton, for instance, he could have done it. But if it was Tynemouth, or Swansea . . . not.'

Easter was standing in front of the fire, one arm along the chimneypiece, her head bent towards the fire and her hair falling across her face. 'I see.'

'I think there's a very big chance that he did it, Easter. He's the sort of person who becomes heavily involved.'

'In what way?'

'In life, I mean. Thoroughly old-fashioned. He lives his life right up to the brim and he feels things so passionately that you can sense his oscillations a mile off. Probably it's partly indigestion. The lining of his stomach is burnt to ribbons, it gives him hell.'

'You're mad!'

'You can see him for yourself. He'll probably be here tonight and you'll meet him. The police are also going to be here, Easter, dear. I hope you don't mind.'

'Not at all,' Easter returned, feebly sarcastic. 'I'll have coffee and sandwiches ready.'

'It will be quite a party,' Nat said thoughtfully. 'But I may be all wrong. Never having met a gipsy before, I may have got him wrong. He may *not* be arriving at Euston this afternoon and be coming straight here to "knock my block off". On the other hand, if I have got him correctly typed, he will. With your permission I am also going to fetch Valentine herself.'

Easter put her hand to her long slim throat. 'Oh, Nat!'

Nat was serious now. 'It's horrible for you, darling,' he said, standing up beside her and putting his arm round her. 'But there's got to be a show-down. It's the only way. If we can *show* the police who murdered the Craggs it's a lot better than simply telling them what we think.'

He looked round. 'We must have them in this room. Do you think we could have that Spanish leather screen you've got in the dining-room, across that corner? We can put the inspector and his mate behind it.'

Easter crumpled down on to the hearth. 'Are we going to have a rough-house?'

'Not for long, if at all. There are going to be police cars in Putney tonight, on the look out for Doxie Lee. You see, he *may* not come to the house.'

'You said he would.'

'I said I *thought* he would. I think he'll come after me because he thinks I've stolen his girl, which, for the sake of argument, I have. Almost certainly his first act on Saturday morning would be to go to my hotel in Liverton-upon-Sands, so I left this address there for him. He couldn't come yesterday as he was playing Liverton, but he could come today, by a slowish Sunday train from the North. When he sees the address Silverdale Number 2, he'll know that I know a lot more than I should. He won't be able to rest or sleep until he's spoken to me and he knows exactly how much I know. And, you know, that old saw about the dog and its vomit isn't altogether an empty cliché. The place where they murdered has an irresistible attraction for some murderers; they've got a compulsion to go back and look at the place where they did it. He's had two good murders, good successful murders, right here. And third time lucky . . .' Easter was sitting on the sofa now, her eyes closed, her head back, her face a deathly white.

'Do I have to be here?' she asked, through a dry mouth.

He used whisky and kindness and a few kisses before he got her back to normal. He made up the fire and he rubbed her cold hands and kissed her cold face. The sun had left the room and now a chilly spring light was filling it. He lighted the lamps and cleared away the tea things and carried in the embossed screen.

'That was one of Jason's wedding presents to us,' Easter murmured as she watched him arranging it across the corner beside the far window. 'It won't be damaged, will it?'

'I hope not.' Nat looked at the clock and at his watch. 'Doxie can't possibly be here before six. I think he'll wait till dusk, somehow. He'll want a meal when he arrives at Euston, too. If he has murder on his mind, he'll wait until it's dark. Blast that daylight-saving hour.'

He sat down again beside Easter and took her hand.

'But my best work,' he said, 'has been on Ernest Millage. I'd make a fine patcher-up of bust marriages. I spent the morning with Ernest Millage pointing out to him the folly of his ways, the folly, that is, of letting his mother have such an influence over him. I've cracked up his Valentine so that he can hardly wait to get her back and start afresh. I haven't lost sight of the idea that he might possibly be a murderer. A simple character on the surface, there are those who would say that he was a far more likely murderer than my flamboyant Doxie. We shall see. We are creating a situation full of possibilities for collisions of temperament. He may give himself away under the stress of emotion. If he does the police will be there to witness it.'

'Where is this Valentine now?'

'She spent the morning in a respectable hotel, the most respectable she has ever stayed in, in Bloomsbury. After my interview in Finchley with Ernest Millage we, that is, Valentine and myself, lunched together in town, and now she is here.'

'Here?'

'Resting in my flat,' Nat said, very slightly smug. 'I shall ring through and tell her to come when I want her. She knows exactly where to come.' Nat cleared his throat. 'Valentine and I understand each other perfectly.'

'How nice,' Easter remarked coldly.

'Valentine,' Nat stated sententiously, 'has her points.' And in order to dissipate any ill-feeling, he took Easter in his arms and buried his face in her sweet-smelling hair.

'Why do you lie to me, Nat? What was the point in telling me that you were divorced?'

'It is perfectly true. My first wife divorced me, our marriage was a flop. Never heard of a man marrying again?'

'Do you love your Swedish wife?'

'Very, very much.'

'Then why do you want to maul me about?'

Nathaniel was not often shocked, but he was shocked now. As he told his wife later his blood ran cold. He disentangled himself and moved across the sofa.

'Because you're a pretty girl.'

'Do you kiss every pretty girl you meet?'

'Nothing like it,' Nat replied cheerfully, 'but that doesn't mean I don't want to. I thought you enjoyed it.'

'Well, I don't,' Easter returned curtly.

'You mean,' Nat said nastily, 'you don't if it's not going to lead anywhere.' He thought for a minute. 'And I don't mean to bed; I mean to the altar, to the registry office.' He looked at her thoughtfully. 'You're respectable, aren't you, Easter?'

'I'm not a tart, if that's what you mean.'

'A nice respectable girl,' Nat said dreamily. At last light was dawning, at last he was beginning to understand Easter. At last he was beginning to see the marriage of his friend York and Easter in the whole. It needed a big effort of imagination, but he could now see York's thoughts turning to his old love, his thoroughly unsuitable, third-rate, superficial, but nevertheless warm-hearted Valentine. He had a glimmer of understanding as to why York could not bring himself to tear up her photograph. Only a glimmer.

CHAPTER XIV

If the inspector and his assistant had accepted drinks the waiting period might have been easier. But the inspector was wondering if some practical joke were being played upon him, and, it being a Sunday evening, he was in no mood to be trifled with and he showed it.

His men were deployed amongst the dark bushes of Silverdale, some of which were now breaking into gaudy flower, the whole division was on the alert and a cordon could be thrown round the house within a few seconds. It was nerve-racking to sit in the sitting-room of the murder house, making desultory conversation and waiting for something which might not happen.

'If Millage comes too soon,' Nat said nervously, 'he'll have to go into the dining-room, and wait, as though waiting his turn at the dentist's. I'd better attend to the front door, Easter. And, Inspector, will you both disappear behind the screen when the bell rings? Oh hell!' Nat exclaimed. 'I'm beginning to wonder now whether I haven't been a complete fool and this extraordinary gipsy chap hasn't upset my judgement.'

The inspector in his well-cut light tweed overcoat was as non-committal as someone who had come to talk about an insurance policy. There was nothing whatever in his manner to show whether he had, or had not, discovered anything significant about Doxie Lee's recent movements. Nat guessed he was probably longing to be back home at his own fireside.

After an hour or so Nat began to sweat with anxiety. Easter sat in a corner of the sofa, making no attempt at conversation, idly turning over the pages of a magazine she must now know by heart. The inspector and his assistant sat, simply sat, not even smoking, taking up space and breathing air but otherwise adding nothing to the gathering. Nat wandered about, in and out, fidgeting with the curtains, attending to the fire and finally, almost defiantly, mixing himself a scotch-on-the-rocks. And another. And almost another, but there was a noise outside like a helicopter arriving in the driveway.

Doxie Lee had come, but by this time Nat's nervous tension was such that he could not produce a smile or a quip; he went, stiffly unsmiling, to the front door.

Yes, Doxie Lee had arrived, but not the way Nat had expected. One of the comedians, whose face Nat vaguely remembered as the drunken Irishman, had brought him in his ancient but distinguished Jaguar. In spite of Sunday's licensing hours they had both had plenty to drink. Both were noisy, blustering and pugnacious and, though they were clearly out for trouble, Nat felt some relief; it was so obviously not the arrival of a man intent upon murder.

The first struggle was to get Doxie to leave his friend outside in the car. Why not get his friend to come back for him later on, Nat suggested. But no, that wouldn't do.

He was the only friend Doxie had left in this hard, cold world, he must come in too. Besides, he might come in useful when it came to getting Valentine out, because get Valentine they would, that's what they'd come for. Doxie, pressed, refused to cross the threshold unless his friend came too so he, Nat, could darn well go and tell that girl to pack her traps and come, otherwise they would wreck the place, and when he said wreck, he meant wreck.

'And make it snappy,' he roared. 'We've been on the go since mid-day and we're driving back to Huddersfield to-night with the woman, so we've no time to stand here jawing. Minnehaha'll be playing Huddersfield tomorrow night — or else.'

'Those sort of tactics don't work these days,' Nat tried to argue, with an uncomfortable feeling that they did. 'She doesn't want to come back to you.'

'She's thrown in her lot with me and it's me she'll stick with, you — you . . .' Doxie thrust his face up, and Nat felt his odoriferous breath upon his own.

'Watch out now, watch out,' came the shrill voice of his friend who had now retreated into his car in an excess of caution.

Doxie knew better now than to start a fight with Nat. He pushed impatiently past him, through the hall and into the lighted sitting-room where Easter sat, the image of domestic felicity, beside the fire. Nat shut the front door and followed him in.

'Now, Mr Lee,' he said briskly, 'shall we let bygones be bygones? This is Mrs Cragg, Mrs York Cragg, Mr Doxie Lee, Easter. How about a drink? Horse's neck? I'm having scotch-on-the-rocks myself.'

If this were the room in which he had committed murder, he seemed hardly interested. Merely uncomfortable. He accepted a drink with alacrity, his manner subtly altered in the presence of the lady. He looked like a cart-horse finding itself in the paddock at Ascot.

He snatched off his cloth cap, he begged pardon, he fumbled with his spotted made-up bow-tie, he cleared his throat, he glared angrily at Nat.

'Let me explain,' Nat said, when he had supplied him with a tumbler of brandy and ginger ale. And in a kindly manner, like a family doctor explaining the situation to the relatives, he accounted for his subversive presence in Liverton-upon-Sands by saying that Ernest Millage had sent him to try to get his wife back, that he had persuaded her to return to her husband and that they were on the point of being reunited. How much Doxie Lee believed him was neither here nor there.

Nat was thinking, with sinking heart: this is the most godawful anticlimax; I've made the most shocking fool of myself. For whereas he had arranged everything so that Doxie Lee would prove himself to be the murderer, here he was, showing quite clearly that he was not.

He sat, with bowed head, sipping daintily at his drink, more in sorrow now than in anger.

Nat looked at his watch; he had told Millage to arrive 'about seven-thirty' and it was now after that. 'Would you like Valentine herself to confirm what I've told you?' he asked.

Yes, he would.

Nat dialled. 'She'll be here in less than five minutes,' he said.

And then Ernest Millage arrived and the sight of him caused Doxie to become as intractable as a bull.

Millage was still aggressively teetotal; he stood uncomfortably beside the door, twisting his hat round and round. He seemed unable to look directly at the gipsy but darted glances at him from time to time. Doxie stared angrily at the little man, muttering in an audible voice subversive remarks like: 'What the bloomin' hell does she see in him? Of all the . . . !'

Then Valentine arrived. She took her cue from Nat and

with the movement of a homing bird and a cry of the Millage to its mate, she flew into her husband's arms. She played it perfectly.

Then, suddenly, everything became extremely confused. Everyone was talking at once and no one was listening to anybody else. Easter sat in the corner of the sofa, looking shrivelled, the magazine still open across her knees. She was the only one who said nothing.

And then the front door bell rang. For a moment Nat could not believe it; had he heard it? It rang again. He ran his fingers distractedly through his hair. It would be Doxie's friend getting impatient.

As if he hadn't enough on hand!

But it was not Doxie's friend. He was waiting in the car, ostentatiously keeping out of trouble's way.

It was a shortish, fair-haired woman dressed in a neat grey coat and skirt, with trim ankles and tidy feet and a worried expression on her face.

'Could I speak to Mrs Cragg, please?'

A lady-help? A dressmaker?

'I'm afraid she's busy at the moment.' This was upheld by the sound of angry voices coming from the half-open door of the sitting-room.

'Can I give her a message?'

'Who are you?'

'I'm a friend of the Cragg family. I. N. S. Wainwright by name.'

'A friend of Sir Jason Cragg?'

'Yes. I'm afraid . . . we're awfully busy at the moment, Mrs . . . er . . .'

'Bacon is my name. I would like to speak to you but I can see you're busy. I've written down my name, in case I couldn't talk to anyone. And I've written down what I've come about.' She dug about in her handbag and brought out a folded sheet of paper. 'Best have these things in black and white. You see, sir, my husband is a constable in the

Metropolitan Police, Putney Division. He's been telling me about this Cragg case and I bin thinking. He's no idea I'm doing this and it would make things very awkward if he knew. So would you mind . . . that is . . . if you could . . .'

'The reward!' Nat exclaimed impatiently. It sounded now as though at any moment fighting would break out behind him.

'Certainly, Mrs Bacon, I'll hand it to the right quarter.'

'No, no!' she exclaimed. 'That's why I brought it here, to show to young Mrs Cragg. Not to the right quarter, please, Mr Wainwright. It's only an idea I had. I don't mind making a fool of myself but I don't want to make a fool of my Sam. I'd never forgive myself if it got out I'd done this. Sam thinks I'm seeing my mum tonight, and I'm off there now . . . Oh, dear, whatever is happening?'

'You'd better move or you'll be mixed up in another murder,' Nat hissed, thrusting the note into his pocket.

Mrs Bacon didn't need to be told twice. She rounded the car parked in the drive and sped out of sight.

So Nat's carefully planned locality of events was used for a common brawl such as could take place outside any public house any Sunday night with the police taking names and addresses and charging both the men to appear at Putney Police Court the following morning.

Doxie shouted a great deal, pointing out that he was billed to appear in Huddersfield the following night and the inspector telling him that he could still do so and Ernest Millage bleating plaintively that he was a teetotaller and had nothing to do with the brawling, that Doxie was an enticer and a so-and-so.

Valentine wrung her hands in the tradition of a woman for whom men are fighting and Easter wrung her hands in anxiety about her wallpaper and the paint round the door.

Finally Doxie flung off angrily with his now considerably sobered friend.

Valentine and Ernest Millage walked away, each supporting the other, to an hotel where Ernest had arranged to stay until he could find somewhere, other than with his mother, for them to live.

The CID were the last to leave, more in sorrow than in anger. The inspector's manner was only faintly reproachful.

CHAPTER XV

Nat slumped into an armchair and held his head in his hands. The fire had died down; the silence in the room after the recent noise was almost palpable.

'Honestly,' Easter said at last, 'I don't know what to make of you. As the only Cragg left I ought to be angry with you. You come crashing in, behaving like some ridiculous amateur detective, under a footling alias, and rip poor York's wretched little private life to shreds. And where does it get you? Exactly nowhere. You've simply made a fool of yourself, and of everybody else.'

'Yes,' Nat agreed, 'I have made a fool of myself, you're right. But not just for amusement, Easter. Listen, the night before Jason died, we dined at his club; I'd just got back from the Middle East and hadn't seen either of the Craggs for a couple of years. Naturally I'd been terribly shocked to hear of York's death and, of course, poor Jason couldn't talk about anything else. Do you blame him? He talked about York's whole life and upbringing, his University career, his business career, his bachelor life, his marriage, you, yes, you at length, and finally, when dinner was over and we were back at his flat in Arlington Street and having a last drink, he took out the photograph of "Mavourneen". He told me about having had copies made and the steps he had taken to trace her and how he'd actually seen the husband that afternoon. He told me about having interviewed the pathologist's assistant and got out of him that a woman could have done the stabbing. In short, he told me everything that was in his mind, and we sat up late discussing the whole thing, with the photograph propped up on the chimneypiece in front of us.'

Nat got up and walked restlessly about the room.

'Well, twenty-four hours later he was dead! It was like a nightmare, Easter. But you know . . . you must know how ghastly the shock was. Probably a lot less bad for me than for you. And once the shock was over, I started wondering . . . what must I do? Well, I couldn't simply go to the police with everything Jason and I had talked over. There was nothing definite, nothing to go on. It was all just talk and . . . supposition . . . surmise . . . guesswork. But all the same, I couldn't leave things like that. I joined my wife and the children in Sweden for a few days and talked everything over with her. We decided that I must go further into things so I left them there with my wife's parents, having rather a good holiday, and I came back here and started snooping. I had luck to begin with, getting the flat in Nero Court. That was a marvellous bit of luck. But if I hadn't done that I should have thought of some other way of getting to know you, probably through the Ramsgates. Buying Jason's old car had nothing to do with it; I had always coveted the dear old thing. I should have tried to buy that anyway. So now you know everything, Easter. It doesn't seem so fantastic and silly now, does it?'

'Then where do we go from here?'

'That's just it. Nowhere, as far as I can see. Dead end. It could be a dismissed employee, someone with a grudge, an unsuspected lunatic, somebody that no one other than Jason and York know anything about.'

Easter got up and shook herself, like a little crumpled cat.

'Let's have some supper,' she said. 'All those awful people

about, all that quarrelling. Ugh, it's been beastly! I'm sure the inspector was annoyed, Nat.'

'I'm sure he was. But I'm not worried about that.'

Nat stared broodingly at the dying fire. Easter started to get supper. She put the low table near the fire, arranged the chairs beside it and went into the kitchen, where Nat could hear her rattling plates and dishes.

He remembered Mrs Bacon and took the folded sheet of paper out of his pocket.

He read:

Evidence at the inquest of Sir Jason Cragg

Police Constable No. . . . Metropolitan Police, Vine Street Division, said in evidence that he had seen and talked to Sir Jason Cragg who had been at the Ritz Arches at about 6.10 p.m., who had told him he was meeting 'someone' at 6.0 who had not turned up.

Porter in block of flats stated in evidence that Sir Jason Cragg had arranged to meet his daughter-in-law at 6.0; he, Sir Jason, had used his telephone to ring through to the house in Silverdale, Putney, to see if she was there. There had been no answer.

Mrs Cragg said in her evidence that she had arranged to meet Sir Jason at *6.30* at the Ritz Arches.

Did Sir Jason arrange to meet *the murderer* in his car in Piccadilly at 6.0? Did he intend to drive to Putney with his daughter-in-law and *the murderer*? Did *the murderer* drive down to Putney with him and murder him when they entered the house? Where was Mrs Cragg between 6 and 6.30?

Nat, his mind full of the recent happenings, did not grasp the significance at the first reading. He read it again.

'What a very curious thing,' he said as Easter spread a

lace-edged supper cloth on the low table. 'Listen . . .' He read it to her.

'Who brought this?' she asked.

Nat told her. 'But is it so, Easter? What time did you arrange to meet Jason?'

'Six-thirty.'

'Are you sure?'

'Of course I'm sure.'

'Couldn't you be mistaken?'

'I could, but I'm not.'

'What exactly did you do in the afternoon?'

'Jill and I had lunch and went to a movie.'

'Where?'

'At the Curzon.'

'Did you have tea after?'

'No . . . yes . . . no . . . I mean . . .'

'It is only a very few minutes' walk from the Curzon cinema to the Ritz. What were you doing between the time the movie came out and meeting Jason? A good hour and a half.'

'I told Jill I was meeting him . . .'

'Yes, but at what time?'

Her eyes were vagrant, roving round the room; she was trying to remember.

'Look, I'll ring through to Jill Ramsgate and ask her. She'll remind you.'

'Wait . . . wait . . .' She was worried, thoughtful. 'I . . . we came out of the cinema at . . . about five . . . Jill was going to meet John at his club and they were dining with friends. I told her I was meeting Jason . . .'

'At six . . . or six-thirty?'

'Oh, what does it matter?'

'It does matter, Easter. Because it means that about half an hour of Jason's time is unaccounted for. He could have met anyone in that half-hour, anyone . . . who could, as

Mrs Bacon points out, have driven down to Putney *with him*. Do try and remember. It might be frightfully important. It's the tiny things that matter in a show like this.'

'We came out of the cinema at five,' Easter repeated woodenly.

'Yes. You said goodbye to Jill, and then what? An hour and a half before you had to meet Jason, at a point about three minutes' walk away . . . What did you do till six-thirty? If you could only remember it would help us, you know.'

'I went into a coffee bar.'

'Ah! Now we're getting somewhere. Which one?'

'Really, Nat. You're carrying this ridiculous detective stuff too far. As a matter of fact I don't remember the name; it was that coffee bar almost opposite the Curzon, in that street turning off Curzon Street up to Charles Street.'

'You were there for an hour and a half, until a few minutes before half past six? Oh, Easter, are you sure? Look, I'll ring Jill, just to get everything straight.'

'Wait . . .' She ran her hand across her now-furrowed brow. 'Oh, Nat! That was an agonizing night. What happened afterwards put everything else out of my mind. I may have sat in the coffee bar for an hour and a half. I don't remember. Can't you understand how awful everything was? You've just told me what a shock you had over Jason's death. How do you think it was for me? I *found* him, lying there. I came into the house and *found* him.' She buried her face in her hands for a moment. 'And now you expect me to account for every moment before the beastly murder. Have a heart.'

'I'm sorry, Easter. Believe me, I'm sorry. But I must get this thing straight. There's something here that isn't right somehow. I can't be satisfied until I've got it straight.'

She looked at him sadly.

She went round the room restlessly. 'There's a smell of people in here,' she grumbled, 'unclean people. That lousy gipsy stank of drink.'

It was now quite dark outside. Easter threw up the sash of one of the windows and drew the curtains across. She drew all the curtains. 'What a ghastly scene,' she murmured, 'if anyone had been looking in!' She looked at Nat again. He sat in the position of Rodin's 'Penseur', his thoughts very far from her and his surroundings.

'An hour and a half,' he muttered, 'one and a half hours. Miss Blockley, Jason's secretary, would know what time he left the office. What time he had to meet you. Yes, Miss Blockley will know.'

Easter went back into the kitchen where, on the table, was the tray already laid with cutlery, plates, glasses. She turned back and called, from the kitchen door: 'Please make up the fire, Nat.'

An uncarved cold roasted chicken stood on its dish on the table. She went slowly towards the table and thoughtfully opened the table drawer. She looked at her row of knives lying neatly in the drawer. She chose a steel knife, a French meat knife, wide at the hilt and narrowing at the point. There was no need to test it, she knew it was sharp. It was the sign of a good cook to keep efficiently sharp knives in her *batterie de cuisine*.

She put the knife on the tray amongst the table cutlery and carried the tray into the sitting-room.

'An hour and a half,' Nat was still muttering as he rose to make up the fire. With the tongs he reached for a piece of coal and put it on, then for another; supporting himself with his left hand on the edge of the chimneypiece he stretched out for a third lump.

'An hour and a half, but listen . . .' he turned slightly and as he did so the first blow misfired. Aimed at the back of his neck it sliced through the material of his jacket across the top of his shoulder, braking on the shoulder blade. The tongs clattered on to the hearth.

He caught hold of her and stared full into her face, her face of pleasure, of delight, of fiendish, unearthly gladness.

'So it was you.' He forced her arms down into the position he had learned. The knife dropped on to the hearth-rug. She laughed wildly. He had to use all his force to get her hands behind her back, but he succeeded, though waves of nausea were weakening him. When they both fell to the floor he was still within reach of the blessed telephone.

'You're hurting me, you're hurting me. You brute!' Kicking forward was no good, she tried kicking backwards, she could not see him now, he was behind her, putting every remaining scrap of strength into holding her with one hand whilst he dialled with the other.

They lay panting together on the floor, like two exhausted animals. 'It's murder,' Nat told the telephone, 'at Two Silverdale. They'll have to ram the front door; no, a downstairs window is wide open! Hurry, for God's sake hurry!'

He dropped the receiver because he could no longer spare the hand to hold it. 'You opened the window so that Doxie Lee could return, or Ernest Millage, or Valentine . . . or so that the police would think they had. Third time unlucky, though. How did you do the impossible? How did you kill Jason? Tell me, tell me . . .'

She was screaming with laughter now; he had never heard her laugh before. A blackness was stealing up and a dizziness was seizing him. Quickly . . . quickly . . .

Nat looked at his own large hands clasping the tiny wrists with their four silver bracelets. He was pressing the bracelets into the skin. Her wrists were like small branches, but willow branches, the strongest, springiest wood known. Willow branches . . .

There was a great deal of darkness and very little reality left when they burst in between the heavy curtains.

'Here's your murderer, Inspector,' she screamed. 'He was going to kill me, but I was too quick for him. Look, there's the knife . . .'

Nat felt a stream as of warm milk flowing round his neck; there was blood on the pale hearthrug, and down below his sleeve blood poured over his hand and over Easter's small hands.

'I think not,' he heard the inspector say, before he became unconscious, 'I think not . . .'

CHAPTER XVI

It was three days before the inspector called at the private wing of St Thomas's Hospital. Nat was lying in extreme comfort with the pleased look of one who has escaped death by millimetres.

'Well, Inspector, have you got everything tied up?'

The inspector looked a little grim. 'What about you?'

'I'm sewn up; twenty-four blessed little stitches have been hemmed into me. It's hard to believe in the strength of those fairy-like wrists, unless you'd like to see my wound!'

'No, thanks,' the inspector said hurriedly. 'I'll believe anything you like to tell me about the strength in those tiny wrists!' He sat down beside the bed. 'When do you think you'll be well enough for the police court proceedings?'

'A week, perhaps? You'll have to ask the house surgeon.'

'Well –' the inspector looked weary – 'we've got our statement. We always do, of course. The murderer's vanity always comes out over the statement. They're all proud of themselves, at heart, they like making their statement. It gives them no end of a kick. If they'd only keep their ruddy mouths shut it would be a lot better for them.'

'How do you mean?'

'I mean, if they'd only refuse to make a statement until they were legally represented . . . it's always the same; when they do, finally, get a lawyer, he groans over the statement and they try to retract, say they want to make another statement, or say that the statement was made under duress. This dame said at first she wouldn't make a statement. Then she thought better of it. She asked for pen and paper and said she'd write it. Well, that didn't do at all. It read like pure fiction. She'd got a wonderful imagination.'

'Funny; she always says she's got none.'

'Believe me, it's marvellous. The imagination she's shown over the planning of the two murders! Just listen to this. That first murder, her husband; it seems it is quite true, he wasn't feeling well that night. It was the six months' anniversary of their wedding, you may remember, there was a small celebration. She says that at that time the marriage had never been consummated; she'd never been in bed with the husband because, her own words: "she didn't want to", she "hated all that sort of thing". When she got back from the theatre with her friends, and let herself into the house, she found her husband had been dosing himself with aspirin and rum, to keep off the flu he thought he was getting. According to her he "started a row" downstairs in the kitchen, where he was boiling the kettle to make himself some more hot grog. He said that if she wouldn't go to bed with him their marriage was a failure, he was going to sue her for restitution and what was more, he wasn't going to spend another night under that roof. He said the position was undignified, he'd rather break up the whole thing, let the world see that his marriage was a failure, than continue to live with her in the circumstances. He went upstairs. She followed him, with the kitchen knife, and as he was getting his travelling-bag out of the wardrobe, she . . . well, you know the rest. After that she turned the central heating up as high as it would go, to keep the body reasonably warm, and went off to bed for a good night's sleep . . .'

'Surely she didn't write all this!'

'She started writing a kind of novelette, like a magazine story, leading up to it. Of course, I couldn't let her. I got everything out of her in one long stream, in the end. All in her own words, not drawn from her sentence by sentence by any means.'

'I can tell you from experience,' Nat put in, 'it wasn't done in a fit of anger. It was done in the coldest of cold deliberation.'

'I believe that. Wait, wait till you hear . . . she began to think, after that, began to be a bit afraid of all the investigation and so on. Afraid that someone might start to think. So what does she do? Provides a first-class red herring. She goes to that photograph shop on the corner of Brewer Street and Sparrow Lane, in Soho, where they sell photographs of stage people; know it? She goes there and buys that glossy photograph for four shillings and sixpence, writes her message on it, and slips it under the paper in her late husband's desk. There's imagination for you,' the inspector said, almost proudly.

'She says she hadn't the slightest intention of murdering her father-in-law, but it seems in the end she "had to". Sir Jason wasn't content to leave things as they were, he insisted on finding out something about the photograph. Apparently actresses can go and have their photographs taken for a nominal sum, at a photographer's of that kind, on condition that the photographer can do what he likes with it. It is good publicity and they can have as many copies as they like for themselves at a low cost. Sir Jason put some thought, care and money into discovering who this woman in the photograph was; it was only a matter of time before he would find out that the hiding of the photograph where he found it was a trick. Everything about his son's death would have been, suddenly, only too clear. So she had to plan Sir Jason's death with some care.'

'In that,' Nat said, 'she did the impossible. I can't think up the answer to that one.'

'Can't you? It is so simple. The boot of that old Rolls-Royce car came in useful.'

Nat remembered the joker at Liverton-upon-Sands who

had got himself into the boot.

'But there were several things she had to do first,' the inspector went on. 'She had to buy plasters and break the cloakroom window, to make it look like forced entry; she had to buy a man's grey plastic mackintosh; she had to prepare the room for a nice little supper party for two; she had to loosen the heel of her shoe; she had to build up an alibi for herself in town. It was that alibi that let her down. It was rotten, rotten! She relied too much on her own perfection, on the fact that no one would ever suspect her. She said at the inquest on Sir Jason that she had arranged to meet him at six-thirty, but, in fact, she told him six, and that I have been able to confirm with the secretary. Between coming out of the cinema about five with Mrs Ramsgate and parting from Mrs Ramsgate, the young lady was very busy. She knew all about Sir Jason's little private car park in the city, and she used it for her own advantage. This murder grew out of existing circumstances, that's where it's so darn clever. She parted from Mrs Ramsgate about five, casually, as people who meet frequently will. First she went to Green Park Station and bought herself a ticket to East Putney. Then she went to the city in a taxi, which she left somewhere near the Royal Exchange. Then she walked to the private car park. She knew damn well that Sir Jason locked his engine, but not necessarily the car itself, unless he had anything in it, an overcoat, a rug or something of the kind, that might be pinched. But in any case, the left-hand window was divided, you will know, so that a slight pressure of the arm would make it open outwards for hand signalling. She knew that by exerting pressure inwards on the chromium at the top of that slip window, on the outside, she could make it swing open outwards and could easily get her hand inside and unlock the door. As it happened she didn't need to; the car was unlocked. She took the T-shaped key out of the leather door pocket, unlocked the boot, put the key back into the pocket, *put on the grey plastic mackintosh* and got into the boot of the car, keeping the lid open a small fraction in order to have fresh air. She did all that in the dark. What a nerve, eh? Things could have gone very wrong. Sir Jason might have opened the boot for some reason. But he didn't. No, sir, he didn't. She says she knew he wouldn't, there wouldn't be any reason to. No, Sir Jason did exactly what she expected him to do. He arrived at the car park about twenty to six, climbed in, drove out, waited for her at the Ritz Arches, got worried about her non-appearance and drove down to Putney at top speed.'

The inspector paused.

'Go on,' Nat urged.

'It's so damned simple that I feel almost ashamed I didn't think of it myself. But it is all built on premise, that premise being that nobody was going to suspect *her*. Now that we know she's guilty, it seems impossible that we didn't. But the fact remains, we didn't. And we never should have. Well, Sir Jason arrived at Two Silverdale, in a minor panic. Jumps out of the car, opens the front door with the keys she knew he had, goes inside and looks round. Finds nothing wrong, comes out and turns out the headlights of the car, goes back into the house. Our heroine climbs stiffly out of the boot, runs round to the back yard, lets herself into the kitchen with the back-door key, picks up the knife she has left ready, the same knife that you know so well, and waits, concealed behind the back lobby door. She knows he's getting ice to fix a drink, and she waits, watching him from the darkness of the kitchen, until he makes up the fire in the sitting-room. She's been successful with stabbing in the back before, she must keep to the pattern. She's kicked off her shoes, now she swoops in as he's making up the fire ... you know the rest.'

'Far from it.'

'Very well ... after that neat bit of butchery she steps out of the mackintosh, leaving it on the floor; she washes the knife in her own spotlessly clean sink, and puts it away in the kitchen drawer with the other knives. Leaving every thing as she found it, she lets herself out of the back door, which she locks behind her, hares off to the main road, catches a bus to Putney Bridge, the stop *before* East Putney on the London side. She's already got a ticket from Green Park to East Putney in her purse. She attracts no attention at Putney Bridge Station, buying a ticket to Wimbledon which she destroys later. She steps out of the train at East Putney, along with other rush-hour commuters, *remembering* to wrench off the heel of her shoe so that she imprints herself upon the memory of the railway staff if ever it should come to a show-down, which, of course, it never would. But just in case . . . Incidentally, she's given up the ticket she bought at Green Park Station. Then into a taxi and up to Silverdale and the body found with the taxi-driver as a witness. And it all worked out exactly as per schedule. I think she thought that was positively her last murder. And it probably would have been if you hadn't come barging in.'

'Oh no! No . . . no . . . you're wrong there! It was Mrs Constable Bacon, your Constable Bacon's missus. It was she who pointed the finger of doubt. I don't think,' Nat said slowly, 'I would ever, ever have suspected her if it hadn't been for Mrs Bacon; and incidentally, Inspector, she must get that Five Thousand Pounds reward. And she deserves it, she's a woman of parts.'

'I will get on to the Craggs' solicitor about that straight away. I'm delighted for Bacon and his missus to have that. Bacon is a good chap, though he lacks inspiration.'

'His wife more than makes up for that.'

'By the way, the family solicitor has been knocked practically out by all this. Mrs Cragg asked him to represent her but when he'd heard a few of the facts he flatly refused. We've got another solicitor now, for her legal aid. He knows that all the Cragg money is at his disposal, he'll get the best counsel there is, Mr L—, I have no doubt. It creates a very curious anomaly, doesn't it? Cragg money used to get her off!'

'But she won't get off!' Nat exclaimed, startled.

'I wouldn't like to say,' the inspector murmured. 'She'll make a lovely show in the witness box. The mourning widow, the sorrowing daughter-in-law.'

The inspector paused, walking over to the window.

'And then there's always the vexed question of insanity. With all that money at the disposal of the defence they may decide to go all out for acquittal on the grounds of insanity and they'll probably get the best psychiatrist for their purpose. He'll stand up there in the witness box and declare she was a psychotic personality. Nobody knows exactly what that is but the magic words will make the jury sit up and take notice, letting the photographs of the stabbed men fall from their fingers.'

He smiled a little wanly. 'I've experienced it so often; I know the form. There'll be a long argument as to the exact definition of psychotic personality, of responsibility, and oblique references to the MacNaughton Rules, and the judge will look his wisest.'

'But she's not "unfit to plead", nor anything like it!' Nat exclaimed.

'No, but what about all that laughter when she was having a go at you? And she's not shown one scrap of remorse. Nor fear of the consequences. Of course, they may decide not to go for the madness plea. They can wipe up her statement and lay stress on her first explanation, when we found her with the knife on the floor between you. You're a sex maniac, they can say, and the minute you were left alone with her you tried to rape her and, in self-defence, she snatched the knife from the supper tray and stabbed you.'

But the inspector laughed at the expression on Nat's face.

'No, I'm pulling your leg; there's too much that goes

before in this particular case. The defence will have to decide what line they are going to adopt after the charge is decided upon; she won't be charged with the attempted murder of you, but the murder, accomplished, of either her husband or Sir Jason Cragg and that will depend upon the evidence available. The weakness lies in the motive and you may be sure the defence will stress that. "What motive had she?" Mr L— will ask. "Why kill her husband?" or "Why kill her father-in-law?" The motive is wispy to say the least of it.'

'You and I don't find it so, Inspector,' Nat declared, 'because we know her. She's a frigid woman all right; marvellously acquiescent up to a point and after that . . . nothing. She's out for material gain only. She didn't kill York because he was going to insist upon his conjugal rights . . . oh no! She could have done that any time during the past six months. She killed him because he was going to leave her, and she found there was nothing she could do to stop him other than . . . what she did. She thought she'd got him and the house and her position as a married woman all tied up and when she found that he really meant to abandon her, and possibly to sue her for restitution, she killed him. There was no planning about that first murder; she did it and then relied upon her own integrity, her acting ability, her iron nerves and her imagination. She knew no one would suspect her, and no one did; did they now?'

'Quite frankly, I didn't.'

'Nor anyone else.'

'And Sir Jason was killed because he stuck his neck out.'

'Yes. He couldn't leave bad alone. And I'm sure she enjoyed that, too. You know, I saw her face when she was attacking me. It is something I shall never forget; I hope I shall never be nearer to Hell. But I believe there is a deep psychological flaw there, shown by the undoubted fact that she liked doing it. Enjoyed it. And when she'd finished she was pleased and stimulated because she'd saved her face in the sight of the world, she was still the respectable and infinitely pathetic widow. If you want the psychological significance you'll have to go to Freud or some other "investigator of the Id by the Odd".'

CHAPTER XVII

Police Constable Bacon beamed at his wife over the top of *Huggett's Weekly Home Finder*. His manner resembled that of a husband who has just been informed that his wife has had triplets: he was proud, pleased and yet slightly puzzled and bewildered.

'When did you really start to suspect?'

'I've known all along,' Mrs Bacon lied. 'Right from the start!'

'Fancy!' PC Bacon was thoughtful.

'Trust a woman's instinct.'

'But you never even saw her! It was only what I told you. I've said all along what a nice little thing she was.'

'Well, it just goes to show.'

'Exactly what?'

'She was a bit too pathetic for my liking,' she extemporized. 'I thought and I thought. And when I read the report I couldn't believe my eyes. Half an hour out, I thought, and not a soul has noticed it! She's got them all eating out of her hand, I thought. Just like men: a pretty face and good measurements, that's all you think about.'

'She's not all that beautiful,' he argued, 'but she was every inch a lady!'